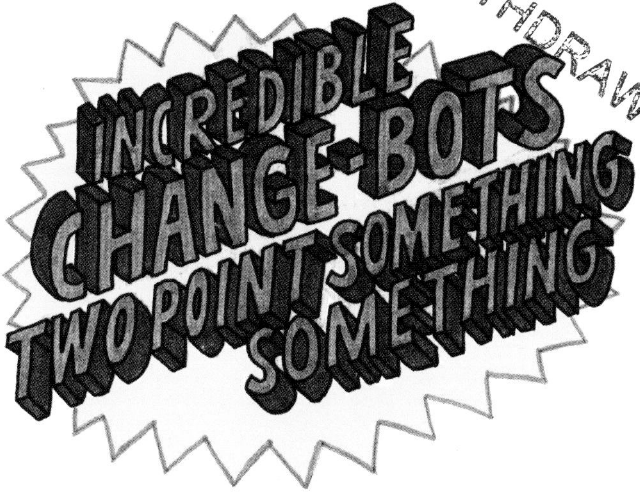

INCREDIBLE CHANGE-BOTS TWO POINT SOMETHING SOMETHING

MORE THAN JUST MACHINES---
VERY, VERY SPECIAL
MACHINES!

PUBLISHED BY TOP SHELF PRODUCTIONS, PO BOX 1282, MARIETTA, GA 30061-1282, USA. PUBLISHERS: BRETT WARNOCK & CHRIS STAROS.

VISIT OUR ONLINE CATALOG AT: WWW.TOPSHELFCOMIX.COM

ISBN 978-1-60309-348-4
1ST PRINTING.
PRINTED IN MALAYSIA.

INCREDIBLE CHANGE-BOTS TWO POINT SOMETHING SOMETHING: ODDS, ENDS AND MISSING PARTS

TABLE OF CONTENTS!

TABLE OF DISCONTENTS

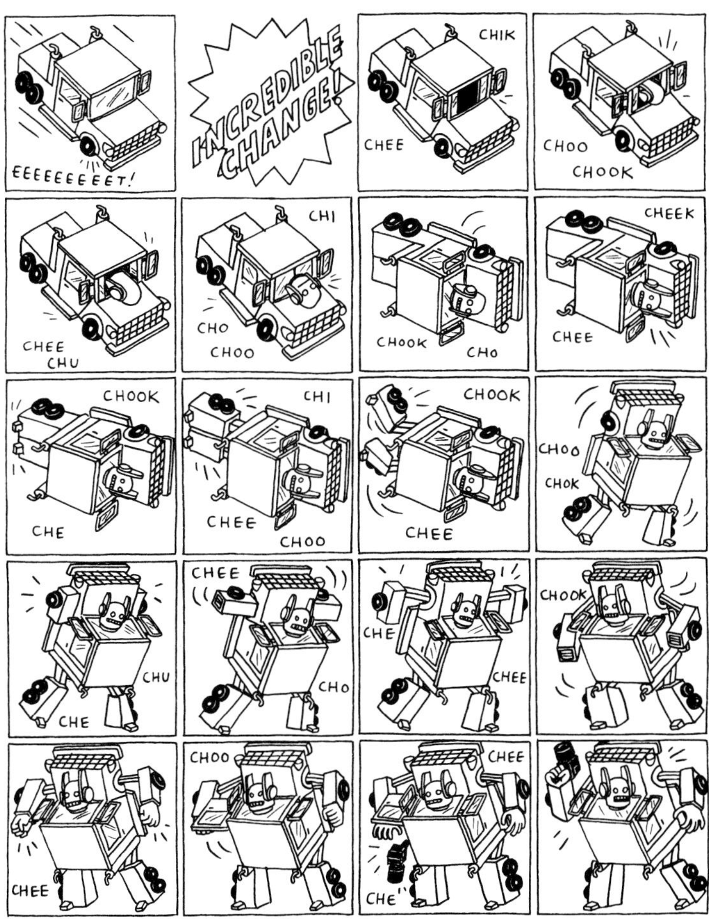
EEEEEEEEEET!
INCREDIBLE CHANGE!
CHIK
CHEE
CHOO
CHOOK
CHEE
CHU
CHI
CHO
CHOO
CHOOK
CHO
CHEEK
CHEE
CHOOK
CHE
CHI
CHEE
CHOO
CHOOK
CHEE
CHOO
CHOK
CHU
CHE
CHEE
CHO
CHE
CHEE
CHOOK
CHEE
CHOO
CHEE
CHE

BDEW!
BEW!

Jeffrey Brown

CHOO
CHEE
CHEE
CHOO
CHOOK
CHOO
CHEE
CHEE
CHOO
CHOOK
CHO
CHOO
CHEE
CHOOK
INCREDIBLE CHANGE!
CHEE
CHOO
CHE
CHOOK
CHEE
CHU
CHEE
CHOO
CHO
CHEE
CHOOK
CHEE
CHOO
CHEE
CHE
CHOOK
CHO
CHOO

FIRST APPEARANCE:
SULK SKETCHBOOK #10
JANUARY 2004

INCREDIBLE CHANGE-BOTS!

YOU SHOULD'VE INCREDIBLE-CHANGED WHILE YOU HAD THE CHANCE!
KLANG!
NOOOO!

BIG RIG'S EARLIEST UNDELETED MEMORY

ELECTRONICYBERCIRCUITRON

Jeffrey Brown

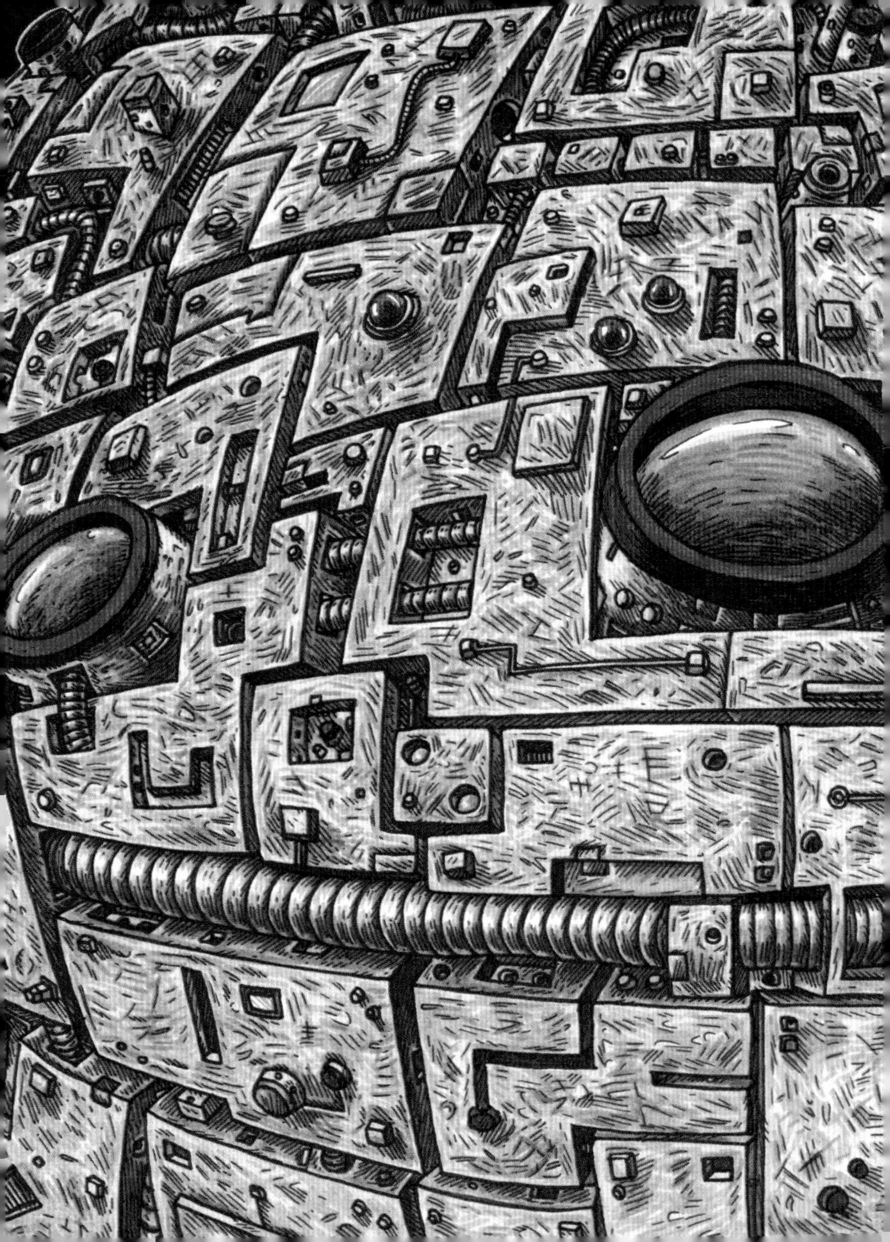

TALES OF ELECTRONOCYBERCIRCUITRON

ON THE HOME PLANET OF THE INCREDIBLE CHANGE-BOTS, THE AWESOMEBOTS STRUGGLE WITH THEIR RIVALS FOR CONTROL OF THEIR WORLD...

THE FANTASTICONS HAVE STOLEN MY COPY OF THE DOMINATING MATRIX OF LEADING!
WE WILL GO TO THEM-- AND TAKE IT BACK!

YEAH!
YEAH!
ALRIGHT!
WAIT, CAN HE STILL LEAD US THERE?

SHORTLY...
RETURN OUR MATRIX!
NEVER!
WHAT MATRIX?

YOU'LL PAY FOR THIS INSULT, FANTASTICONS!
OW!
BDEW!
OH, WAIT A MINUTE!
HERE IT IS! IT WAS IN MY CAB!
SORRY ABOUT THAT, EVERYBODY.
JERK.
FIN

Young
RUST
I DON'T KNOW!

THE START OF SOMETHING
WOW! THAT CHANGE-BOT LOOKS REALLY CUTE.
DOO DEE DOO DEE DOO

I'VE GOT TO COME UP WITH A GOOD MOVE TO TALK TO HER...

OOPS!
OH!
BUMP

OH MY GOSH! I'M SO SORRY! ARE YOU OKAY?
YEAH, I'M OKAY.
CHEE CHOO
CHE CHOOK
CHEE CHOO
INCRED-IBLE CHANGE!
CHEE CHOO-CHOOK

MY NAME'S HONKYTONK.
I'M SIREN.

UM ... CAN I GIVE YOU A RIDE HOME OR SOMETHING?

TURNING ON AND OFF
AND THIS IS MY BEDROOM...
SO... THIS IS WHERE YOU SLEEP AT NIGHT, HUH?
YEAH. HEH.
WAIT!
OH!
I'M SORRY. IT'S TOO SOON, I KNOW... NOW I'VE MESSED IT ALL UP...
NO, THAT'S NOT IT...
I JUST WANTED TO TURN THESE LIGHTS OFF FIRST.
OOOOOHHH
CLICK

LATELY
SO, WHERE'S THIS SIREN YOU'VE BEEN SEEING?

UM, SHE SHOULD BE HERE SOON...

WEE OOO WEE OOO
WEE OOO

I WASN'T SURE YOU WERE COMING.
I HAD A FLAT.

BRRRRRRR.

MAKE BOTH

WATCH OUT!
BEW!
BEW!
BEW!
BEW!

THANKS... THAT WAS CLOSE!
ARE YOU AS TURNED ON AS I AM?
LET ME CHECK MY DIAGNOSTICS.

YES.

KLANG
KLANG
KLANG
KLANG
KLANG
KLANG
KLANG
KLANG

DIFFERENT DIFFERENCES
HEY!
SIREN?

HOW HAVE YOU BEEN?
PRETTY GOOD.
THAT'S GOOD. WELL, I GOTTA RUN, BUT IT WAS GOOD TO SEE YOU.
OH, OKAY.

WHO WAS THAT?
THAT WAS RUSTY. WE...USED TO GO OUT.

YOU DATED A FANTASTICON?!
IT WAS A LONG TIME AGO.

YOU DIDN'T EVEN INTRODUCE ME.

SAY THE RIGHT THING
SO, HOW ARE THINGS WITH SIREN?
BEW! BEW!

THEY'RE... GOOD.
BEW!
WAIT, WHY'D YOU HESITATE?
BEW!
BEW!

I DON'T KNOW, THINGS ARE GOOD BUT THERE'S SOME THINGS THAT MAKE ME WONDER IF IT'S RIGHT...
BEW!
BEW!
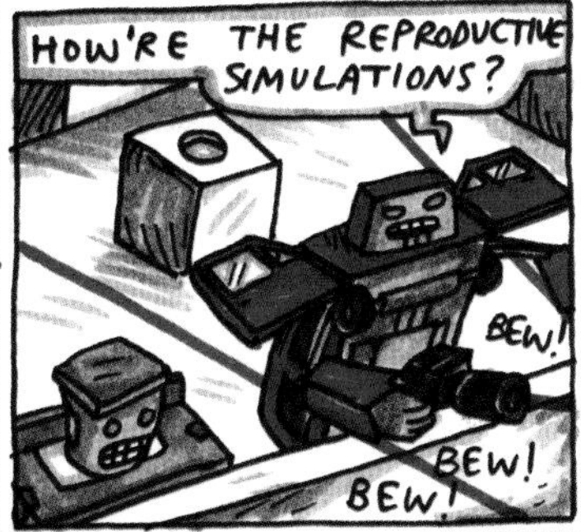
HOW'RE THE REPRODUCTIVE SIMULATIONS?
BEW!
BEW!
BEW!

VERY MECHANICAL AND SCIENTIFIC.
BEW!
SO IT'S GOOD?
YEAH, IT'S GREAT.
BEW!
BEW!
BEW!

SO WHAT'S THE PROBLEM?
BEW! BEW!
BEW!
BEW!
BEW!

HAPPY ANNIVERSARY
IT'S NICE TO RELAX LIKE THIS FOR A BIT, NOT HAVE TO WORRY ABOUT FIGHTING...
YEAH..
SO, I HAVE SOMETHING FOR YOU
WHAT IS IT?
OPEN IT
WHERE DID YOU GET THIS?!
ACTUALLY, I MADE IT.
I... I LOVE IT.

NEW TIRES
I'M GOING OUT WITH SOME FRIENDS. HOW DO I LOOK?
OH.

YOU GOT NEW TIRES.

WHAT? DO THEY LOOK FUNNY?

NO, YOU LOOK REALLY NICE.

WHAT'S THAT SUPPOSED TO MEAN?

NOTHING. NEVER MIND.

I LOVE YOU.

BEW!

BEW!

BEW!

BEW!

RAZOW!

I LOVE YOU TOO.

I HAVE TO TELL YOU SOMETHING
HONKY, UM, CAN I TALK TO YOU?
YEAH, OF COURSE, WHAT IS IT?

THIS IS KIND OF HARD TO SAY...
IT'S OKAY. YOU CAN TELL ME.

I THINK I'VE GOT SOME RUST. DOWN THERE.

BUT...HOW...I DON'T HAVE ANY... WHERE DID YOU GET SOME RUST?

I DON'T KNOW?

BAD NEWS
OKAY, YOU CAN GO AHEAD AND INCREDIBLE CHANGE FOR ME.

WE'LL NEED TO WAIT FOR THE TEST RESULTS, BUT IT LOOKS LIKE RUST.
INCREDIBLE CHANGE!
CHEE
CHOO
CHEE
CHOOK

UM, I DON'T WANT TO BE A JERK, BUT I KIND OF NEED TO USE THIS ROOM...

HOPE
IT'S OKAY.
YOU KNOW WHAT?

DON'T WORRY, WE'LL GET THROUGH THIS.

THIS IS JUST A LITTLE BUMPS.

I MEAN, NOT BUMPS. ER, AN OBSTACLE. WE JUST NEED TO GET PAST IT.

WE'LL GET THROUGH THIS, RIGHT?

DRIVEN
HEY
HEY
I'M GOING FOR A DRIVE.
INCREDIBLE CHANGE!
CHEE
CHOO
CHEE
CHOO

QUESTIONS
WHAT DID YOU WANT, SIREN?

THIS IS KIND OF PERSONAL, BUT... HAVE YOU HAD ANY PROBLEMS WITH RUST?

OH, SURE, JUST BECAUSE MY NAME'S RUSTY, YOU ASSUME I HAVE RUST! YOU'VE GOT SOME NERVE!

SO... HAVE YOU?

THIS IS UNBELIEVABLE!

AVOIDING CONFRONTATION
AUGGHH*!
BEW!

NICE SHOT.
THANKS.

IT WAS REALLY GOOD HOW YOU, YOU KNOW, TARGETED THAT GUY'S HEAD AND EVERYTHING...

ARE YOU EVER GOING TO TALK TO ME AGAIN?
YES. NO. I DON'T KNOW.

DISTANCE MAKES THINGS FAR AWAY
FELLOW AWESOMEBOTS, THANK YOU FOR COMING.

OUR ESCALATING WAR WITH THE FANTASTICONS IS TAKING ITS TOLL...

HOWEVER, I BELIEVE IN THE END, WE WILL EMERGE VICTORIOUS...

BECAUSE WE ARE PROBABLY RIGHT.

AND SO, I URGE YOU TO CONTINUE FIGHTING AS HARD AS INCREDIBLY POSSIBLE.

FIGHT WELL, MY AWESOMEBOTS, FIGHT WELL!

TIME
WHAT YOU NEED IS SOME PERSPECTIVE.
BEW!
BEW!
BEW!

YEAH, THAT'S A GOOD POINT.
JUST TAKE SOME TIME, YOU KNOW?
BEW!
BEW!

BEW!
BEW!
BEW!
BEW!
BEW!

WOULD YOU MIND SHOOTING BACK AT THE FANTASTICONS FOR A MINUTE HERE?
BEW!
BEW!

HUH? OH, SORRY.
BEW!
BEW!
BEW! BEW!

WAITING ROOM

SIREN?

WELL, THE TEST RESULTS ARE BACK, AND IT'S POSITIVE.
POSITIVE?!
OH, I MEAN, IT'S GOOD NEWS.

YOU DON'T HAVE RUST. IT LOOKS LIKE IT'S JUST SOME OIL OR GRIME OR SOMETHING.

SEE? JUST SOME...
SCRAPE SCRAPE SCRAPE

SOME DIRT OR SOMETHING THERE. BUT NOT RUST... WHAT IS IT THOUGH? I DON'T KNOW... ANYWAY...

ALLS WELL

HEY RACEY
HEY, HONKYTONK. HEY... SIREN.

ER... I'LL SEE YOU GUYS LATER

YOU DIDN'T TELL HIM ABOUT... YOU KNOW...
WHAT? NO, UH, OF COURSE NOT.

BUT STILL AMONGST THE DEVASTATION...

AT THE AWESOME BASE...
HEY, RACEY, WHAT'RE YOU DOING?
WE'RE REPAIRING THE VEHICLE OF OUR HUMAN FRIEND, JIMMY JUNIOR.
FASCINATING!
INCREDIBLE CHANGE!
CHEE CHOOK
CHU CHEE CHO
CHEE CHOO

I'M AFRAID THIS TECHNOLOGY MAY BE TOO PRIMITIVE FOR US.
CRUNCH
UH--

YES, I THINK THIS SIMPLE MACHINERY IS BEYOND REPAIR.
OIL CHANGE

HEY HONKYTONK, LOOK AT ME, I'M A FANTASTICON!
FANTASTICONS?! WHERE?!
BEW! BDEW! BEW!
HEY!
WHAT THE HECK, BIG RIG? CHILL OUT!
MY CAR
OH, UH, WAIT... UH... WHAT?
UM, I'M GOING TO GO CHECK THE DATA LOGS FOR, UM, YOU KNOW... HEY! KEEP UP THE GOOD WORK!

BALLS

MEANWHILE, AT THE AWESOMEBASE...
SO, HOW DID YOU GET YOUR NAME, BALLS?
MY NAME? I GUESS IT WAS ASSIGNED TO ME ON THE DATE OF MY MANUFACTURE.

OH. I THOUGHT MAYBE IT WAS BECAUSE YOU'RE A GOLF CART.
"GOLF?" WHAT IS "GOLF?"

IT'S A GAME PLAYED HERE ON EARTH. YOU USE CLUBS TO HIT LITTLE BALLS INTO LITTLE HOLES!

THAT SEEMS PRETTY SIMPLE. SO IT'S A CHILDREN'S GAME?

NO, IT'S FOR ADULTS. IT CAN BE PRETTY HARD.. THERE'S HILLS AND, YOU KNOW, SAND PITS AND THINGS...

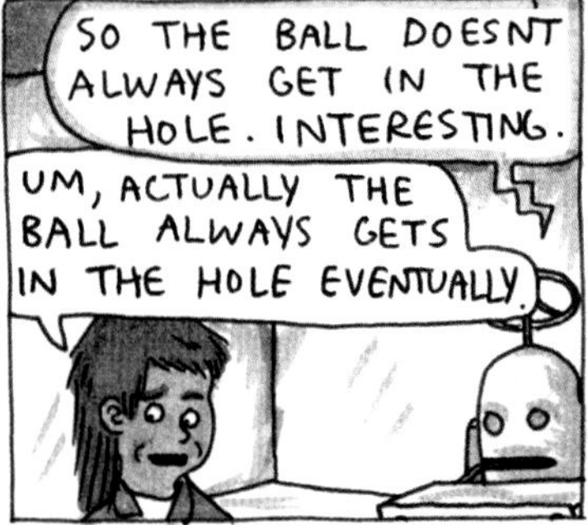
SO THE BALL DOESN'T ALWAYS GET IN THE HOLE. INTERESTING.
UM, ACTUALLY THE BALL ALWAYS GETS IN THE HOLE EVENTUALLY.

OH. HM. AND WHERE DOES THE CART COME INTO PLAY? FOR SCORING?
UM, NO, JUST FOR DRIVING FROM HOLE TO HOLE.

I DON'T GET IT.

INCREDIBLE CHANGE!

CHEE CHOO CHEE CHOOK CHU CHEE CHOO

LET'S GO, JIMMY JUNIOR!

HOWEVER, AS BALLS AND JIMMY JUNIOR HEAD OFF, OMINOUS FIGURES WATCH FROM A HIDDEN BUNKER!

WITH EAGLE-EYE AIM, BALLS SHOOTS A HOLE IN ONE OF HIS FOES

AND DROPS THE SECOND BOGEY WITH A CHIP SHOT

FINALLY, THE FANTASTICONS RETREAT, NO MATCH FOR THE HAZARD PRESENTED BY THE ROUGH AND READY AWESOMEBOT!
DID YOU GET THEM? I COULDN'T GET MY LASER TO WORK.
YOU'VE GOT THE SAFETY ON THERE.
OH.
RAZOW!
OOP-
CLICK
SORRY.

MICROWAVE
SOUPY AND POPPER

MEANWHILE, AT THE FANTASTICON MEGACAVE...
FANTASTICONS! I'VE CALLED YOU HERE FOR A VERY SPECIAL MISSION!
WE NEED A MASTER OF DISGUISE TO INFILTRATE THE AWESOME BASE.
AREN'T WE ALL BASICALLY "MASTERS OF DISGUISE."?

YES, BUT FOR THIS MISSION, WE NEED A VOLUNTEER, BECAUSE OF THE EXTREME DANGER.

THIS IS MY SPECIALTY, SHOOTERTRON. I'LL DO IT.
EXCELLENNNNT.

YOU WON'T ABANDON ME THERE LIKE LAST TIME, WILL YOU?

UM, NO. OF COURSE NOT.

SOUPY! POPPER! GET IN!

AND SO...
I DON'T THINK THIS IS THE RIGHT PLACE.
QUIET!
SOUPY! RECONAISSANCE MODE!
YOU MEAN GET OUT AND LOOK AROUND?
YEAH.

EEEEEEKKKKKK!
AAAHHHHHH!
EEEEKKKKK!
AAAHHHH!
EEEEKKK!
AAAHHH!
WE'VE BEEN COMPROMISED!

WE'LL HAVE TO FIGHT OUR WAY OUT! GET BACK IN, SOUPY!
AAAHHHH!
BEW! BEW!
CRASH!
SHOOTERTRON, WE'VE BEEN DETECTED! REQUEST IMMEDIATE EXTRACTION!
SHOOTERTRON?
COME IN?

A BRIEF HISTORY OF THE TIME I MADE AN OFFICIAL INCREDIBLE CHANGE-BOTS FAN CLUB

THE FIRST CHANGE-BOTS FAN CLUB COST TWENTY DOLLARS. YOU GOT A MINICOMIC, MEMBERSHIP CARD AND A FULL COLOR CHANGE-BOTS DRAWING. I MADE EACH DRAWING AS A "MISSING PANEL", WHICH I ARRANGED INTO A KIND OF STORY FOR THIS COLLECTION. THE SECOND VERSION OF THE FAN CLUB COST FIVE DOLLARS, FOR WHICH YOU RECEIVED A NEWSLETTER, A SMALL DRAWING IN BLACK AND WHITE OF YOUR FAVORITE CHANGE-BOT, AND A MEMBERSHIP CARD. THE MATERIAL FROM THE NEWSLETTERS IS ALSO COLLECTED HERE. I WOULD CONTINUE THE FAN CLUB OFFER, BUT IT'S TOO MUCH WORK, ALTHOUGH I'VE CONTINUED TO OFFER IT AT SELECT SIGNINGS AND CONVENTIONS, AS LONG AS I STILL HAVE SOME OF THE HAND LETTER-PRESSED MEMBERSHIP CARDS LEFT.

-JEFFREY BROWN, 2012

INCREDIBLE
CHANGE-BOTS
FAN CLUB
OFFICIAL MEMBER

INCREDIBLE
CHANGE-BOTS
FAN CLUB
OFFICIAL MEMBER

WHAT DO YOU MEAN YOU DON'T UNDERSTAND THE BATTLE PLAN? YOU GUYS GO ATTACK OVER THERE, AND YOU GUYS GO ON THAT SIDE, AND THEN YOU GUYS SWITCH OVER TO WHERE THE OTHER GUYS WERE GOING, AND THEN I CRUSH THEM IN MY HAND LIKE INSECTS! IT'S SIMPLE.
Jeffrey Brown

WHO WANTS ME TO SHOOT THEM? LET'S SEE HANDS.
Jeffrey Brown

I'M GONNA SMOKE YOU!
Jeffrey Brown

IT'S TIME TO DO WHAT I DO BEST -- SHOOT THINGS!
Jeffrey Brown

AS SHOOTERTRON IMAGINES HIS VICTORY, HE BEGINS TO LAUGH FIENDISHLY TO HIMSELF...
HEH HEH HEH HEH HEH HEH HEH HEH HEH HEH!
Jeffrey Brown

IF ONLY SHOOTERTRON REALIZED HOW USEFUL MY CEMENT-MIXING ABILITY IS! THEN I'D BE HIS FAVORITE.
Jeffrey Brown

DAMMIT, SOUPY, GET OUT OF THERE!
NOT UNTIL YOU APOLOGIZE!
Jeffrey Brown

OH MY GOSH! SOUPY, ARE YOU CRYING?
NO! I'M LEAKING! GET ME A TOWEL.
Jeffrey Brown

OKAY, GUYS, GET BACK IN HERE. AND YOU BETTER START BEHAVING INSIDE THERE!
Jeffrey Brown

GET OUT OF HERE, BALLS!
OH! SORRY
Jeffrey Brown

DON'T CROSS ME, OR I'LL CALCULATE YOU! I SWEAR I WILL!
Jeffrey Brown

BUT IF BIG RIG IS MY FATHER, THAT MEANS SHOOTERTRON IS--
HE'S, LIKE, YOUR COOL UNCLE.
Jeffrey Brown

THE TIME FOR TALKING IS OVER! NOW, IT IS TIME TO DANCE!
Jeffrey Brown

THE OTHER AWESOMEBOTS WAIT PATIENTLY AS OLD TIMEY SLOWLY INCREDIBLE-CHANGES...
HERM
INCREDIBLE CH...
CREEEEEEK
REEEET
EEEKKK
EEEEEEKK
CREEKK
Jeffrey Brown

DON'T GIVE ME ANY LIP! I'VE BEEN INCREDIBLE-CHANGING SINCE BEFORE YOU WERE CONSTRUCTED!
Jeffrey Brown

WHEN I WAS YOUNG, WE DIDN'T GET TO INCREDIBLE-CHANGE. WE HAD TO HAVE A MECHANICBOT COME, DISASSEMBLE US, AND THEN RE-ASSEMBLE US IN VEHICLE FORM!
Jeffrey Brown

IT'S NOT MY FAULT I FORGOT! DATA STORAGE TECHNOLOGY WASN'T AS ADVANCED WHEN I WAS CONSTRUCTED.
Jeffrey Brown

LET'S CLEAN UP THIS MESS!
NO, REALLY, SOMEONE LEFT A WHOLE BOX OF JUNK OVER HERE AND IT'S KIND OF IN THE WAY.
Jeffrey Brown

OH, WATCH YOUR STEP OVER THERE..
WHAT? OH, GROSS! GOSH DARN IT, STINKY!
SORRY.
SPLURTCH
Jeffrey Brown

FINE, I'M LEAVING! BUT YOU'LL FEEL BAD WHEN THERE'S A BIG BATTLE AND YOU GUYS ARE OVERPOWERED AND I COME IN AT THE LAST MINUTE AND TOTALLY SAVE YOU AND STUFF!
Jeffrey Brown

HEY, WHAT WAS THIS DOING IN THERE? IT'S NOT GARBAGE.
Jeffrey Brown

AND SO THE AWESOMEBOT REMAINS OBLIVIOUS AS MICROWAVE AND HIS EASYSERVE MINIONS HATCH THEIR PLAN!

GIGGLE SNICKER

SHHHHH! BE QUIET!

Jeffrey Brown

WHILE THE AWESOMEBOTS SLEEP, POPPER EMERGES FROM HIDING TO EXPLORE THE AWESOMEBASE...
Jeffrey Brown

GO, SOUPY AND POPPER! ATTACK, MY LITTLE FRIENDS!
RARRRR!
I WISH HE'D GIVE US GUNS...
Jeffrey Brown

BEW!
WATCH OUT!
BEW!
BDEW!
BEW!
BEW!
BDEW!
BEW!
Jeffrey Brown

AT MICROWAVE'S COMMAND, POPPER RELEASES HIS DEVASTATING ATTACK!
RARRR!
POP!
POP!
POP!
POP!
POP!
POP!
POP!
POP!
POP!
WHAT THE--?! AW MAN, IT'S GETTING ME ALL GREASY!
POP!
Jeffrey Brown

ALL RIGHT, FANTASTICONS, GET READY TO BE SHOT BY BALLS!
Jeffrey Brown

HOWEVER, THE SEEMINGLY INNOCENT LETTERPRESS MACHINE IS ACTUALLY THE AWESOMEBOT KNOWN AS.. IMPRINT!
INCREDIBLE CHANGE!
CHEE
CHOO
CHU
CHE
CHEE
CHOOK
CHEE
CHOO
Jeffrey Brown

SURROUNDED ON ALL BUT ONE OR TWO SIDES, MICROWAVE AND HIS DIMINUTIVE FRIENDS MAKE THEIR FINAL STAND!
BEW!
BDEW!
BEW!
BDEW!
BEW!
BEW!
BEW!
BEW!
Jeffrey Brown

SOUPY! POPPER! QUIT STRIKING DRAMATIC POSES AND GET BACK IN HERE! IT'S TIME TO GO.
BDEW!
BEW!
BEW!
Jeffrey Brown

I DIDN'T KNOW TODAY WAS TRASH DAY!
IT'S NOT. TRASH DAY WAS YESTERDAY.
WHATEVER.
KLANG!
Jeffrey Brown

WITH A LOOK OF GRIM DETERMINATION, RACEY REALIZES WHAT HE MUST DO...
I MUST STOP THE FANTASTICONS!
UM, YOU GUYS CAN HELP ME.
Jeffrey Brown

IN AN INSTANT, BALLS EXPLODES INTO ACTION, READY TO BATTLE!
CHEE
CHOO
CHE
CHEE
CHOO
CHOO
CHOOK
CHE
CHEE
CHOO
INCREDIBLE CHANGE!
Jeffrey Brown

FORTUNATELY, HEADLIGHT'S UNIQUE TALENT SHOWS THE AWESOMEBOTS WHERE THEIR ENEMIES ARE HIDING...
THERE THEY ARE!
Jeffrey Brown

BALLS! IS THAT YOU?
AHHHHH! I'M BLIND! I'M BLIND!
Jeffrey Brown

HEY, GET YOUR FINGER OUT OF THERE!
WHAT THE--?!
Jeffrey Brown

ONCE AGAIN, STINKY IS UNABLE TO SNEAK UP ON THE FANTASTICONS...
DAMMIT!
WHA--?!
KLANG
KLANG
KLANG
Jeffrey Brown

¡YEARGGHH!
¡RARRRR!
BOEW!
RAZOW!
Jeffrey Brown

Hey Guys, look! I can shoot stuff while I'm running!
BEW! BEW!
Jeffrey Brown

TAKE THAT, YOU JERKS!
BEW!
BOEW!
Jeffrey Brown

LEAPING FROM THE CLIFF, AFTERBURNERBOT SUFFERS FROM A MOMENTARY LAPSE OF CERTAINTY...
OH, WAIT, WE CAN STILL FLY IN ROBOT MODE, RIGHT, GUYS?
BDEW!
WHAT?!
BEW!
JeFFrey Brown

AAAGGHH! DAMMIT, WHY DO YOU GUYS ALWAYS SHOOT ME FIRST?
BANG!
RAZOW!
Jeffrey Brown

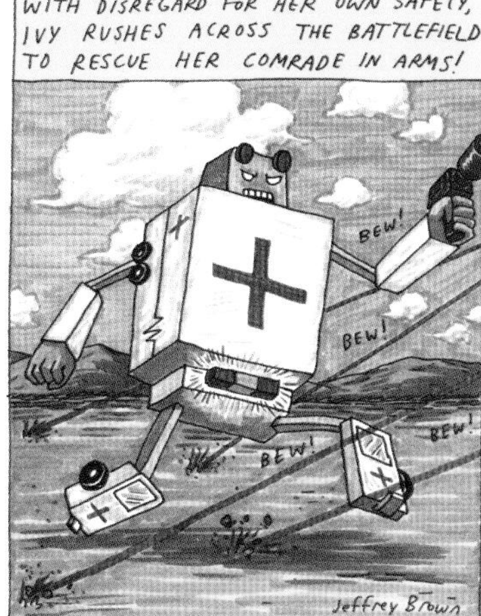
WITH DISREGARD FOR HER OWN SAFETY, IVY RUSHES ACROSS THE BATTLEFIELD TO RESCUE HER COMRADE IN ARMS!
BEW!
BEW!
BEW!
BEW!
Jeffrey Brown

SORRY, I WOULD'VE GOTTEN HERE SOONER BUT I FORGOT TO INCREDIBLE-CHANGE AND ENDED UP RUNNING THE WHOLE WAY.
Jeffrey Brown

UNABLE TO SAVE THE FALLEN AWESOMEBOT, AND WRACKED WITH GUILT, IVY FLIES INTO A MURDEROUS RAGE!
BEW!
BDEW!
BEW!
NOOOO!
Jeffrey Brown

DEFTLY EVADING INCOMING FIRE, PAPERCUT FIGHTS BACK WITH LASER EYES!

RAZOW!

BDEW!

OW! HEY!

Jeffrey Brown

HONK! HONK! HONK!
HEY! STOP LAUGHING AT MY BATTLE CRY!
BDEW!
Jeffrey Brown

ENRAGED, HONKYTONK TOSSES THE DIMINUTIVE FANTASTICON ASIDE!
YEARGGHH!
AIEEE!
Jeffrey Brown

I WILL DEFEAT YOU--- WITH MY EXTREME FORESHORTENING!
Jeffrey Brown

DON'T WORRY, HONKYTONK, I'LL SAVE YOU!
BDEW!
BEW!
BUT I'M FINE.
Jeffrey Brown

STINKY! BALLS! COVER ME!
WE'VE GOT YOU COVERED, BIG RIG!
Bew!
Bew!
BDEW!
Jeffrey Brown

I'M TIRED OF FOLLOWING YOU TO VICTORY!
I'LL STILL COME, BUT I JUST HAD TO SAY HOW I FEEL.
Jeffrey Brown

WITH UNEXPECTED GRACE, BIG RIG AVOIDS THE INCOMING LASER BLASTS!
BDEW!
BEW!
RAZOW!
BEW!
BEW!
BEW!
BDEW!
Jeffrey Brown

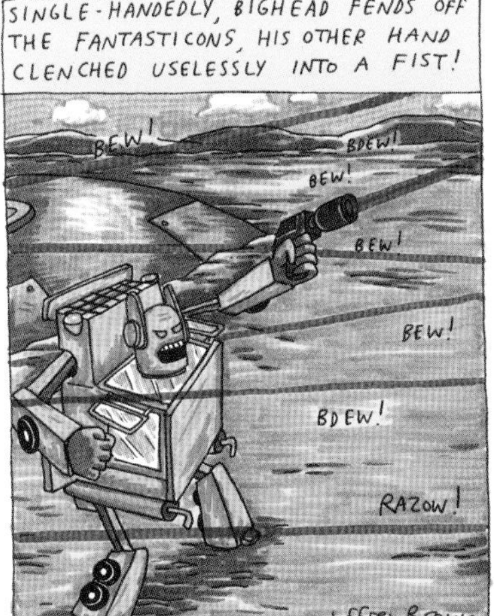
SINGLE-HANDEDLY, BIGHEAD FENDS OFF THE FANTASTICONS, HIS OTHER HAND CLENCHED USELESSLY INTO A FIST!
BEW!
BDEW!
BEW!
BEW!
BEW!
BDEW!
RAZOW!
Jeffrey Brown

ALTHOUGH BIG RIG DOES NOT MANAGE TO ACTUALLY SHOOT ANY OF THE FANTASTICONS, HE DOES LOOK IMPRESSIVE.
RAAAAGGGGHHHH!
BDEW!
BEW!
RAZOW!
BEW!
BDEW!
Jeffrey Brown

WITH SHOOTERTRON OUT OF THE WAY, I, AFTERBURNERBOT, CAN LEAD THE FANTASTICONS--TO AVENGE SHOOTERTRON!
BEW!
Jeffrey Brown

MAYBE WE COULD SPLIT INTO TEAMS, AND I COULD LEAD ONE OF THE TEAMS?
NO.
Jeffrey Brown

YOU'D NEVER UNDERSTAND!
OR I'LL SHOOT YOU!
Jeffrey Brown

EJECT UNLEASHES HIS HIDDEN WARRIORS UPON THE FANTASTICONS!
RARRR!
STEGGY! BUZZY! ATTACK!
BZZZ
CHOO! CHEE!
CHEE! CHOO! CHEE! CHOOK!
CHEE! CHOO!
Jeffrey Brown

AND SO, AS THE BATTLEFIELD ERUPTS INTO A FIERY INFERNO, AFTERBURNERBOT TAKES TO THE SKIES AND ESCAPES!
HA HAA!
WOOOSH!
Jeffrey Brown

HEY, LOOK, UP IN THE SKY! IT'S A PLANE! NO, IT'S A ROBOT! NO, WAIT, IT IS JUST A PLANE.
Jeffrey Brown

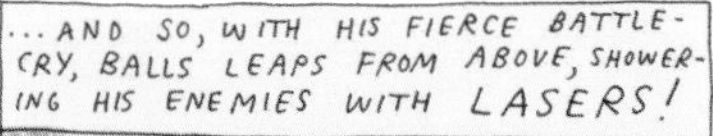
...AND SO, WITH HIS FIERCE BATTLE-CRY, BALLS LEAPS FROM ABOVE, SHOWERING HIS ENEMIES WITH LASERS!

WAHHHHHHHHHHNNHH!
BEW!
BDEW!
Jeffrey Brown

STUNNED, THE FANTASTICONS WATCH BALLS DROP DOWN ON THEM WITHOUT WARNING!
WHA--?!
BEW!
BDEW!
RAZOW!
Jeffrey Brown

MY HAT! YOU HEARTLESS BASTARDS, YOU'LL PAY FOR THAT!
BEW!
BDEW!
Jeffrey Brown

I'M GONNA GIT YOU!
I'M GONNA GIT YOU ALL!
AND THEN I'M GONNA GIT YOU AGAIN!
BEW!
BDEW!
BEW!
BEW
Jeffrey Brown

HEARTBROKEN, BUT ONLY PARTIALLY DISILLUSIONED, HONKYTONK RAMPAGES THROUGH THE USED CAR LOT!
DIE, FANTASTICONS, DIE!
BEW! BEW!
GRE
FANTASTIC PRICE!
Jeffrey Brown

HEY, BIGRIG, I THINK I FOUND YOUR GUN, BUT, UM, YOU'LL HAVE TO DIG IT OUT...
Jeffrey Brown

FEELING REFRESHED, STINKY PREPARES TO HEAD BACK INTO BATTLE...
Jeffrey Brown

I'LL SHOW YOU FANTASTICONS HOW TO SORT YOUR TRASH INTO THE PROPER BINS-- WITH MY LASER GUN!
BEW!
Jeffrey Brown

AND SO, STINKY ADDS INSULT TO THE INJURY OF THE FALLEN FANTASTICON.
MAYBE I SHOULD RECYCLE THIS FOR AWESOMEBOT REPLACEMENT PARTS...
MY LEG!
Jeffrey Brown

AS OLD TIMEY STANDS OVER HIS DEFEATED FOE, HE SILENTLY CURSES THE SENSELESS WAR HE FINDS HIMSELF FIGHTING IN...
CURSE THIS SENSELESS WAR!
Jeffrey Brown

CAN YOU INCREDIBLE-CHANGE BACK INTO A CAR? I WANT TO SHOOT YOUR TIRES OUT.
NO!
Jeffrey Brown

IF I WANTED YOUR OPINION, I'D DOWNLOAD IT FROM YOUR MEMORY FILES AFTER I SHOOT YOU, JERK!
Jeffrey Brown

AS HE LAYS DOWN HIS COVERING FIRE, CEMENTOR BEGINS LAYING THE FOUNDATION FOR A DEFENSIVE STRUCTURE...
WHIRRRRRRRRRRRRR
BDEW!
BEW!
Jeffrey Brown

VALIANTLY, HOSER CONTINUES TO FIGHT!
YOU WON'T TAKE.. URG.. ME.. ALIVE.. COUGH COUGH
BEW!
BEW!
Jeffrey Brown

AS THE BATTLE RAGES, OLD TIMEY AND BALLS FORMULATE THEIR PLAN!
WE'RE PINNED DOWN! WHAT SHOULD WE DO?
THIS REMINDS ME OF THE TIME I WAS JUST A YOUNG AWESOMEBOT, AND... WAIT, WHAT WERE WE TALKING ABOUT?
BEW!
BEW!
BEW!
Jeffrey Brown

OH, HOLD ON, THIS THING IS STILL SET ON "LASER"...
BEW!
BEW!
Jeffrey Brown

BRAVELY, RACEY DEFENDS HIS FALLEN COMRADE FROM THE FANTASTICONS!
IF YOU WANT HONKYTONK, YOU'LL HAVE TO GO THROUGH ME FIRST!
BEW!
BEW!
I'M OVER HERE, RACEY
BEW!
BEW!
Jeffrey Brown

UNFORTUNATELY, SHOOTERTRON'S ANGST OVER THE BURDEN OF LEADERSHIP GOES UNSEEN BY THE AWESOMEBOT HE HAS JUST BLOWN AWAY...
WHY MUST YOU MAKE ME DESTROY YOU? WHY?
RAZOW!
Jeffrey Brown

AND SO, BALLS MOURNS THE DEATH OF HIS FRIEND...
YOU GUYS WILL PAY FOR THIS!
Jeffrey Brown

REST EASY, OLD FRIEND...
YOU WILL BE AVENGED!
Jeffrey Brown

IN THE MIDST OF FIGHTING, BALLS BEGINS TO PONDER THE BIG QUESTIONS...
IS THIS REALLY ALL THERE IS TO BATTLE? SHOOTING AT EACH OTHER?
BEW!
BEW!
BDEW!
BEW!
Jeffrey Brown

BALLS?! WHAT'S WRONG?
ENH, I'M KIND OF BORED.
BEW!
BEW!
BEW!
BDEW!
BEW!
Jeffrey Brown

HEY GUYS, I FORGOT SOMETHING AT THE AWESOME BASE. I'LL BE BACK IN A MINUTE.
BEW!
BDEW!
BEW!
Jeffrey Brown

ALRIGHT, YOU GUYS WAIT RIGHT THERE! I'LL BE BACK TO SHOOT YOU LATER!
BEW!
BEW!
BDEW!
Jeffrey Brown

WITH A SIGH OF RESIGNATION, BALLS DECIDES TO REJOIN THE BATTLE
I GUESS I BETTER GET OUT THERE AND SHOOT STUFF.
Jeffrey Brown

HEY GUYS, ARE YOU DONE SHOOTING STUFF? BECAUSE I'M BACK NOW. IS THERE ANYONE WE STILL NEED TO SHOOT?
Jeffrey Brown

RETURNING TO BATTLE, BALLS SHOWS A LOT OF GUTS!
C'MON, GUYS! LET'S GET THEM!
BEW!
BDEW!
BEW!
BEW!
BDEW!
Jeffrey Brown

ONCE AGAIN, ARSONAL FINDS HIMSELF IN THE LINE OF FIRE-- AND EXPLODES INTO FLAMES!
YEAGGGHHHHH!
BEW!
BDEW!
BEW!
BAM!
Jeffrey Brown

I'M TIRED OF SHOOTING AT YOU GUYS.
I'M GOING HOME.
Jeffrey Brown

WITH HIS FRIEND SERIOUSLY DAMAGED, JIMMY JUNIOR RUSHES TO DEFEND THE INJURED BALLS!
BEW!
BDEW!
BDEW!
ZZZTT
ERG
BEW!
Jeffrey Brown

I'M SORRY, BALLS, I HAVE NO IDEA HOW TO FIX THESE.
DANG IT.
Jeffrey Brown

I'M LEAVING! YOU'RE NOT GOING TO HAVE BALLS TO KICK AROUND ANY MORE!
Jeffrey Brown

FINE! I'M LEAVING! YOU WON'T HAVE BALLS TO KICK AROUND ANYMORE!
Jeffrey Brown

SO, WHAT, I'M A JOKE TO THEM, AM I? I'LL SHOW THEM-- I'LL SHOW THEM ALL!
Jeffrey Brown

AS THE FANTASTICONS CARRY ON WITH THEIR TASKS, THEY REMAIN OBLIVIOUS TO HEROIC BALLS INFILTRATING THEIR MEGACAVE...
Jeffrey Brown

SENSING DANGER, WHEEEEE READIES HIMSELF FOR BATTLE!
Jeffrey Brown

AS THE BATTLE RAGES, WHEEEEE HATCHES A NEW PLAN...
YES, THAT'S IT... INSTEAD OF SHOOTING SHOOTERTRON IN THE BACK, I'LL LET THE AWESOME-BOTS DESTROY HIM FOR ME!
BDEW!
BEW!
BEW!
Jeffrey Brown

SHOOTERTRON PAUSES, REFLECTIVELY...
IS THIS ALL THERE IS? SHOOTING THINGS? IS THIS ALL MY LIFE WILL AMOUNT TO?
Jeffrey Brown

I WILL NOT SPARE CHANGE-BOTS OF ANY FACTION! I WILL HAVE MY REVENGE!
Jeffrey Brown

HOW IT ALL STARTED

When I was in high school, I had the music soundtrack to the Transformers animated movie, the one with the "You got the Touch!" song. Some friends of mine saw and started making fun of it - "What's on that tape? Sixty minutes of CHEE CHOO CHEE CHOO CHOOK?" Years later, thinking about those sound effects inspired the first Incredible Change-Bots drawing in my sketch book.

DID YOU REALIZE?

One of the Incredible Change-Bots is actually a transformer --- that's right, the Fantasticon Sparky is a transformer, a static device that transfers electrical energy from one circuit to another through inductively coupled conductors (according to Wikipedia). He was based on one of the top Google image results from the time he was first created in 2006.

THEME SONG

Back in 2007 when the first Change-Bots book came out, I did an interview with Pirooz M. Kalayeh and ended up writing a Change-Bots theme song which he recorded. You can listen to it online:

http://shikow.blogspot.com/2007/06/interview-with-jeffrey-brown-may-21st-11.html

It includes a video with Pirooz's friend Robert dancing. Check it out!

DID YOU REALIZE?

On page 43 of Incredible Change-Bots (Book One), there's a panel of BigRig talking about how the Fantasticons vanished "into thin air." That panel is a nod to the book cover of Jon Krakauer's "Into Thin Air." I haven't even read that book, actually, so I'm not sure why I put that in the book, except that I saw that cover a lot working at Barnes & Noble.

COLLECTIBLE VINYL BALLS

Chicago comics publisher Devil's Due started making plans to produce vinyl toys in 2008 and made a deal to make Change-Bots toys. The designs were turned into prototypes, the packaging was designed and toys of Balls and Microwave were listed in the Diamond Previews Catalogue --- only to have the whole deal fall apart before production.

DID YOU REALIZE?

On page 68 of Change-Bots Book One, Arsonal says "Thanks for fixing me up, Monkeywrench!" and Monkeywrench says, "That's okay!" This sequence is actually from a Transformers comic written by my brother Doug when we were kids. It became a favorite of ours over the year, one of us saying those lines to the other and we'd both laugh and laugh.

THE LAST WIZARD

Before the first Change-Bots book came out, the August 2007 Wizard (#190) featured an exclusive one page Change-Bots comic. The second Change-Bots book was going to be previewed in Wizard with another exclusive comic, but Wizard announced the end of its print magazine. Fortunately, the Change-Bots appeared in that final March 2011 issue (#235).

DID YOU REALIZE?

In Change-Bots One, on page 110-111, Big Rig collapses in the desert, seeing a vision he at first thinks is the recently deceased Honkytonk, but turns out to be Tredz. This sequence is a shout out to The Empire Strikes Back, when Luke Skywalker collapses in the snow and sees Obiwankenobi. So it's also, like, a statement on hot/cold, real/unreal and stuff.

BAD DREAMS OF BALLS

Balls and Microwave were the first Change-Bots to make cameos in another comic book series. In issue #18 of Tim Seeley's series Hack/slash, the two Change-Bots are amongst a number of characters who appear in the character Vlad's nightmare.

DID YOU REALIZE?

The steering wheel on top of Balls's head is a peace sign? Rather than a hippie reference or antiwar statement, I wanted Balls to reflect the realities of a gray world, not a black and white one. Balls would love to have peace, of course, but is drawn into fighting and as a realist has no illusions about the possibility of lasting peace.

KICKING ASS

In the 2010 film adaptation of the Mark Millar/John Romita Jr. comic book series "Kick-Ass," a poster of the cover to Incredible Change-Bots (Book One) appears on the wall of the cafe at about the 32:30 mark. Look for it below and to the right of the TV.

DID YOU REALIZE?

I have a habit of making the humans have bad plays on words for names. General Deeyer is a corruption of the phrase "General Idea", while Stanley from Change-Bots Book Two has a pretty basic name - he runs Dard farms, so he's Stanley Dard --- standard.

ANIMATED ACTION!

When animator Oren Mashkovski read Change-Bots, he was inspired to write and ask about creating a Change-Bot cartoon. He created a one minute trailer for the Change-Bots, which you can watch online at: http://www.topshelfcomix.com/changebots-trailer/

DID YOU REALIZE?

On page 61 of Change-Bots Book Two, Shootertron refers to "our plans," to which General Deeyer corrects "your plans," and which Shootertron reiterates as "our plans." This was inspired by David Lynch's film adaptation of DUNE, where the Mentat Piter says "our plans" and the Baron says "MY plans" and Piter says "THE plans." It's all about taking credit, whereas in the Change-Bots it's about avoiding responsibility

ADVENTURE BALLS

Although there is no official organization or government for the Change-Bots Fan Club, there is a vice-president: Pen Ward, creator of the awesome cartoon AdventureTime. Pen's favorite Change-Bot? He likes Balls. As VP, he has zero actual responsibilities.

DID YOU REALIZE?

When Macrowave appears on page 128 of Change-Bots Two, Balls exclaims "He's too Big too exist!" This is a nod to Mark Beatty, who runs the local comic shop in my neighborhood, DarkTower Comics. Mark is over six feet tall, and his grandma used to tell him he and his brother were too big to exist.

www.darktowercomics.net

ALMOST FAMOUS

Although there has been some interest from film and TV studios in developing the Incredible Change-Bots, nothing definite has happened. There was a shopping agreement in place with ████████ ████████, including animator ████████████████ but so far, nothing has come to fruition...

DID YOU REALIZE?

In Change-Bots Two, Shootertron argues about danger with General Deeyer, who claims "You may find that there is danger behind the other danger." The phrase "Danger behind the other danger" is something my son Oscar, who was three at the time, said while playing with some toy animals.
(Page 60 of Change-Bots Two)

EXCLUSIVE PREVIEWS

In addition to a new exclusive comic drawn for Wizard Magazine, the websites Comics Alliance and Comic Book Resources ran exclusive preview strips. There was also a new "Blue Balls" strip (drawn for colorist Bill Crabtree) that was to run in Vice Magazine, and a special ad in the Diamond Previews Catalogue.

DID YOU REALIZE?

On page 98 of Change-Bots Two, Honkytonk and Siren talk about their relationship, and Siren's need for T.L.C.- Total Logistical Control. That phrase is something I've seen on semitruck trailers while driving to Kansas. So I guess it's an actual company. I don't know what they do, but I like their name.

THE ART OF CHANGE-BOTS

To coincide with the release of Incredible Change-Bots Two, the Scott Eder Gallery in Brooklyn held an art show with all the artwork from the book as well as a number of new pieces created specifically for the art show.

DID YOU REALIZE?

The sequence at the top of page 107 in Change-Bots Book One was inspired by (and so gives a nod to) cartoonist Sammy Harkham's story in the Drawn & Quarterly Showcase Book 3, called "Somersaulting", where the characters are setting off fireworks and one says "I want to live forever."

BALLS PATROL!	DID YOU REALIZE?
Inspired by the classic sidescrolling arcade game "Moon Patrol," the computer game "Balls Patrol" is hours of pointless entertainment, programmed by fellow Chicagoan Dan Henrick.	Although I don't watch nearly as much reality TV as I used to, I still managed to reference it a bunch in Change-Bots Two. Agent Recog is based on the TV show Cheaters' host Joey Greco, while Shootertron's team of lawyers is based on TV judges, led of course by a stand in of Judge Mathis, my favorite.

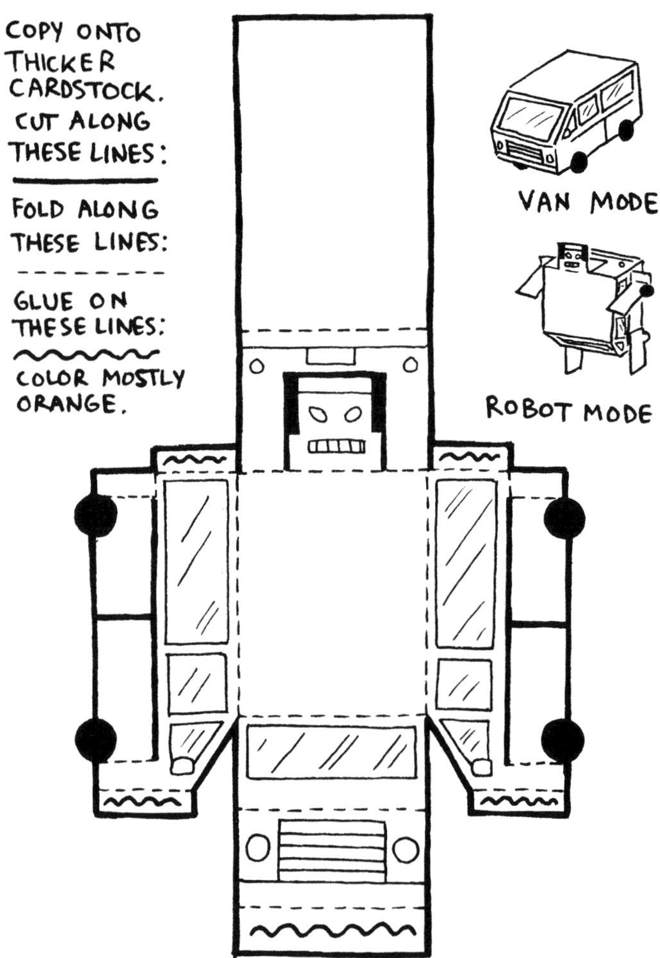

INCREDIBLE CHANGING RUSTY CUTOUT

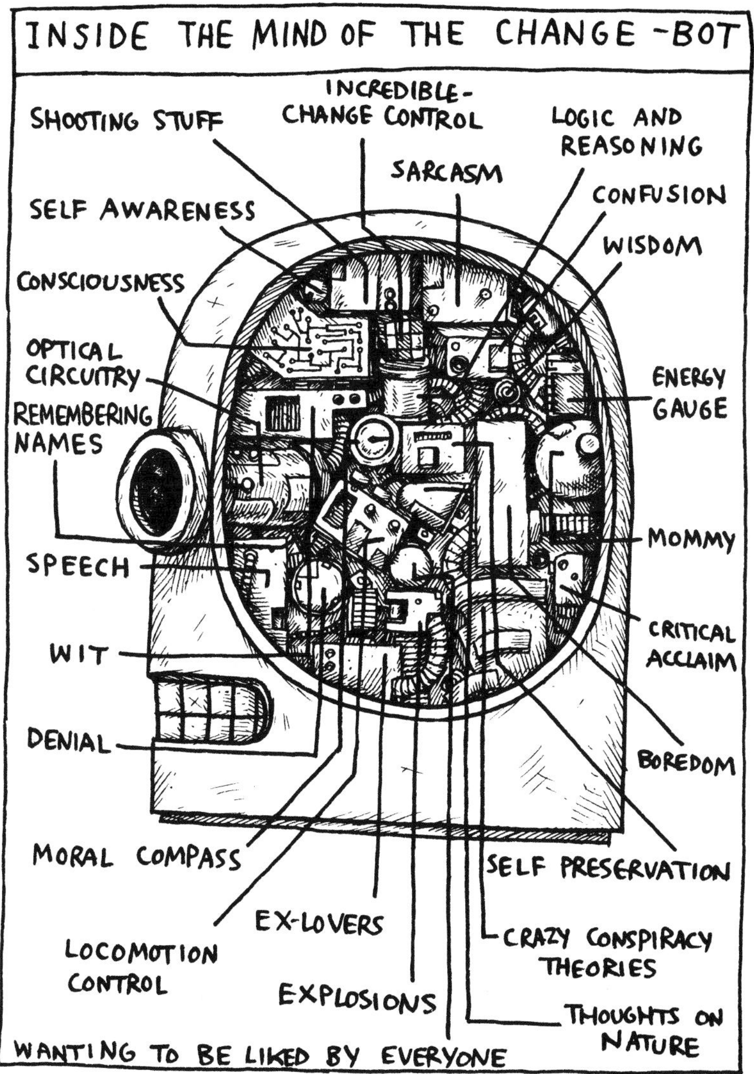
INSIDE THE MIND OF THE CHANGE-BOT
SHOOTING STUFF
INCREDIBLE-CHANGE CONTROL
LOGIC AND REASONING
SARCASM
CONFUSION
SELF AWARENESS
WISDOM
CONSCIOUSNESS
OPTICAL CIRCUITRY
ENERGY GAUGE
REMEMBERING NAMES
MOMMY
SPEECH
CRITICAL ACCLAIM
WIT
DENIAL
BOREDOM
MORAL COMPASS
SELF PRESERVATION
EX-LOVERS
LOCOMOTION CONTROL
CRAZY CONSPIRACY THEORIES
EXPLOSIONS
THOUGHTS ON NATURE
WANTING TO BE LIKED BY EVERYONE

BUILD YOUR OWN CARDBOARD MICROWAVE TOY!

You will need:

- one shoe box
- five rolls of toilet paper
- scissors
- tape
- black marker
- adult supervision

1. Remove toilet paper from cardboard rolls and discard the toilet paper.

2. Remove shoes from shoe box. Discard shoes.

3. Use TP roll to measure holes in shoebox - one on top, one on each side and two on bottom

4. Cut holes out of shoe box.

5. cut one TP roll in half. Insert and tape into top hole.

6. Insert and tape remains 4 TP rolls into other 4 holes.

7. Cut rectangle out of top of shoe box.

8. Tape one side of shoe box lid on to shoe box

9. Draw face, hands and Microwave buttons

10. Use Microwave soup and popcorn for Soupy and Popper!

INCREDIBLE CHANGE-BOTS PEN BATTLEFIELD!

Make copies of battlefield. Taking turns, choose a Change-Bot to shoot. Once a change-Bot is shot, it may no longer battle. Last Change-Bot standing wins.

Balance pen (blue or red for each team) with tip on ChangeBot.

Push pen down across paper to "shoot" enemies.

HOW TO DRAW A BALLS BUST
1
2
3
4
5
6
7
8
9
10
11

Look and Find Traffic Jam!
Can you find all twenty change-bots---
BEFORE THEY TAKE OVER THE WORLD?!

BREAK DOWN YOUR CARDBOARD BOXES--- IT HELPS IF SOMEONE IN YOUR HOUSEHOLD IS O.C.D.
DON'T BREAK DOWN YOUR GLASS BOTTLES, THAT'S DANGEROUS, NO MATTER HOW MUCH FUN.
RECYCLING TIPS WITH STINKY!
HAVE SEPARATE BINS FOR GARBAGE AND RECYCLING. IT'LL BE CLEANER TO SORT.
DO NOT USE RECYCLING ITEMS FOR A CRAFT PROJECT. WHEN IT'S TIME TO THROW IT OUT, THEY'LL BE UNRECYCLABLE

MOTORCYCLE SAFETY WITH WHEEEEEE*
* For entertainment purposes only, please
ALWAYS WEAR A HELMET!
OHHHH, MY HEAD...
ALTHOUGH IT IS POSSIBLE FOR HEAD INJURIES TO TURN YOU INTO A GENIUS, IT IS EXTREMELY UNLIKELY.
I'LL BET I CAN TELEPORT NOW!
MAKE SURE YOUR MOTORCYCLE IS NOT TOO LARGE FOR YOU.
C'MON, MAN, LET'S GO.
OR TOO SMALL.
OW.
ALWAYS MAKE SURE TO SIGNAL OTHER DRIVERS WHEN YOU'RE ABOUT TO TURN.
Bewl
KABOOM!
Bewl
Bew!
PAY ATTENTION, AND AVOID DISTRACTIONS!
HEY, WHEEEEEE! GUESS WHAT?
WHAT?
KLANG!

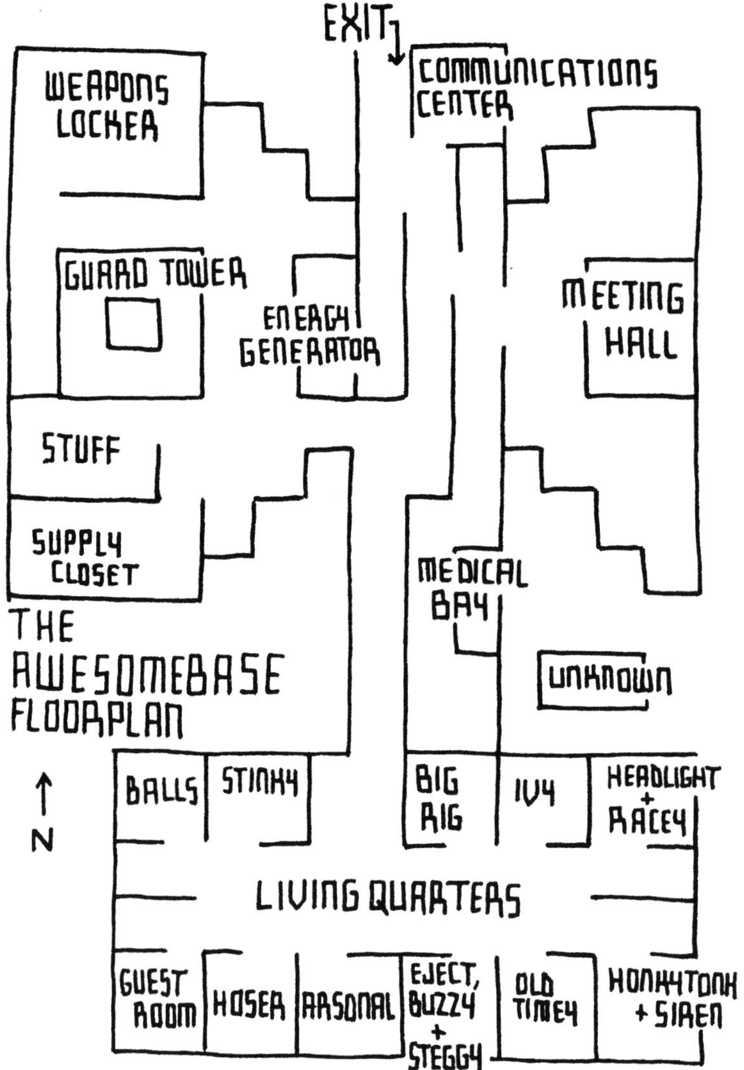
EXIT
WEAPONS LOCKER
COMMUNICATIONS CENTER
GUARD TOWER
ENERGY GENERATOR
MEETING HALL
STUFF
SUPPLY CLOSET
MEDICAL BAY
THE AWESOMEBASE FLOORPLAN
UNKNOWN
N
BALLS
STINKY
BIG RIG
IVY
HEADLIGHT + RACEY
LIVING QUARTERS
GUEST ROOM
HOSER
ARSONAL
EJECT, BUZZY + STEGGY
OLD TIMEY
HONKYTONK + SIREN

Ask Honkytonk and Siren

Dear Honkytonk and Siren,
I've noticed that my girlfriend has "wandering eyes" -- she's always checking out other guys! Should I be worried?
Sincerely, Insecure

DEAR INSECURE,
WORRIED? NOT AT ALL! YOU ARE FORTUNATE TO HAVE SUCH A VIGILANT PARTNER. DANGER CAN STRIKE FROM ANYWHERE. PERHAPS YOU COULD BE LESS LAZY AND KEEP WATCH YOURSELF!

Dear Honkytonk and Siren,
My boyfriend is pretty selfish. He doesn't pay attention to my needs, or even listen to me. I do a lot for him, but he rarely shows me any kind of thanks. How can I get him to think about me more?
Sincerely, Unappreciated

DEAR UNAPPRECIATED,
IT SOUNDS LIKE YOUR BOYFRIEND IS DARK AND BROODING. PERHAPS HE IS STRUGGLING WITH HIS PREPARATIONS FOR BATTLE? OR MORE LIKELY, HIS DARK SECRETS MAY CONTAIN THE KEY TO SOME APOCALYPTIC SCENARIO. BEST NOT TO TAKE UNDUE RISK, SO CONTINUE SERVING HIM--- ALL OUR FATES MAY DEPEND ON IT!

Dear Honkytonk and Siren,
We had a dinner party last week and my wife got in an argument with me in front of our guests. How can we make it up to them?
Sincerely, Embarrassed

DEAR EMBARRASSED,
YOUR GUESTS KNEW WHAT THEY WERE GETTING INTO, AS YOU AND YOUR WIFE CANNOT HIDE YOUR TURBULENT PASSION. IF ANYTHING, THEY SHOULD BE PROBABLY BE THANKING YOU FOR THE SHOW.

THE PHYSICS OF CHANGE-BOTS!

WITH DR. INFALLIBLE

Many people question how it is possible that Incredible Change-Bots are able to change from a vehicle form, that appears to have a certain mass, into a robot form that appears to have an entirely different mass. First, clearly this does not violate any laws of physics, as some of my colleagues have claimed, because it is happening. Second, it is only impossible by the standards of our own inferior technology. It simply requires massive amounts of energy to correctly and, one would assume, safely manipulate the bonds of matter to enable such alterations in apparent mass. This naturally explains the Incredible Change-Bots insatiable desire for new energy. One might ask why the Change-Bots haven't adopted the use of nuclear power; this perhaps relates to some unknown instability created by the demands of the aforementioned apparent mass differences. I've asked some of the change-Bots about all this and they don't seem to understand what I'm talking about.

THE INCREDIBLE CHANGE-BOTS THEME SONG

CHANGE-BOTS, INCREDIBLE CHANGE-BOTS
FIRST THEY'RE ROBOTS, AND THEN
YOU TURN AROUND AND THEY'RE
VEHICLES
DRIVING ALL OVER THE PLACE

CHANGE-BOTS, INCREDIBLE CHANGE-BOTS
CHEE-CHOO-CHE-CHOO-CHOOK
SHOOTING EACH OTHER IN THE FACE

ROBOTS FROM A DISTANT PLANET
COME TO EARTH AND MAKE A
MESS OF IT
CHANGE-BOTS,
INCREDIBLE CHANGE-BOTS!

BEW BEW BDEW BEW

HEY, WHAT DO YOU THINK OF MY NEW TIRES?
THOSE ARE, PRETTY, UH, COOL...
YEAH, THEY ARE PRETTY COOL, AREN'T THEY?

HEY TREDZ, CAN I TALK TO YOU A MINUTE?
NO.
OH, UH, WELL, I JUST WANTED TO--
YEAH, I SAID NO.
BUT... UH...
NO.
AWKWARD.

SHOOTERTRON?
WHAT ARE YOU DOING IN THERE?
OH MY GOSH! LOOK, A ALIEN!
WHAT? WHERE?!
RAZOW!

HEY GUYS, WHAT'S UP?
OH, HEY HONKYTONK!
JUST HANGING OUT... YOU KNOW.
UH... OKAY, SEE YOU GUYS LATER...
SEE YA
BYE
OH MAN!
I KNOW, CHECK IT OUT!

HEY RUSTY, HOW'S IT GOING?
OH MAN, DID YOU HEAR ABOUT GASSER? CRAZY, RIGHT?
ALRIGHT, I GOTTA RUN, BUT GOOD TO SEE YOU, MAN!
INCREDIBLE CHANGE!
CHE
CHEE
CHOO
CHO
CHEE
CHOOK
CHOO
IDIOT.

BEW!
BEW!
BEW!
BEW!
BEWFFT
PFTT
WHAT THE---?!
BEW!
BEW!
BEW!
CLICK
CLICK
CLICK
BEW
BEW!
MAYBE THE SAFETY IS ON?
THAT'S IMPOSSIBLE...
BEW!
BEW!
BEW!
CLICK
CLICK
CLICK
THESE THINGS DON'T HAVE SAFETIES.

HEYGUYS
HEY, BUSHWACKY.
YOUGUYS GOTTATRY THESE SOLAR PANELS
SERIOUSLY IT FEELS SOGOOD MAN
UM, YEAH, MAYBE SOMETIME...
GOTTATRYTHEM
ALRIGHT, BUSHWACKY, WE'LL SEE YOU LATER.
YEAHLATER
SOOOOOOOOOGOOD

MICROWAVE! MY MOST TRUSTED SPY! I HAVE AN IMPORTANT MISSION FOR YOU!
OF COURSE, SHOOTERTRON.
IT WILL MAKE USE OF YOUR MOST IMPORTANT TALENTS. YOU CAN HANDLE IT?
YES, SHOOTERTRON, I'M READY, WHATEVER THE MISSION MIGHT BE!
I NEED YOU TO FIND OUT...
WHAT TIME IT IS!
HA HA HA HA!

JITTERS! WAKE UP!
HUH?
SHOOTERTRON WANTS TO TALK TO YOU. GO MEET HIM IN THE EAST HALL.
WHAT? OKAY, HOLD ON.
INCREDIBLE CHANKK!
CHEE CHOO CLANG
CLANG
CRUNK
WHAT THE--?!
HA HA HA
SNICKER
OH, C'MON GUYS, THAT'S NOT FUNNY! GET THIS THING OFF OF ME!

TAP TAP
UM, WHAT YOU GOT THERE, EJECT?
IT'S A GRAPHING CALCULATOR.
TAP TAP
TAP TAP TAP
SO, UH, WHAT'S -- WHAT DOES IT DO?
OH, IT DOES ALL KINDS OF STUFF, IT'S GREAT.
ALL KINDS OF FUNCTIONS, DOES CALCULAS AND OTHER ADVANCED MATHEMATICS...
OH.
WANT TO TRY IT OUT?
OH, NO... THAT'S OKAY. NO THANKS.
TAP TAP

"YOU'VE CHANGED."

"STINKY, YOU NEED TO START BRUSHING BETTER... YOU'VE GOT SOME PLAQUES IN THERE."

INTERVIEWS
WITH SELECT CHANGE-BOTS
CONDUCTED BY
MR. JEFFREY BROWN

AN INTERVIEW WITH HEADLIGHT

WHAT DOES CHANGE MEAN TO YOU?
IT MEANS A BRIGHTER FUTURE.

THINGS ALWAYS GET BETTER IN THE FUTURE, RIGHT?

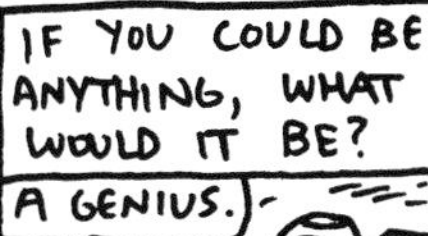
IF YOU COULD BE ANYTHING, WHAT WOULD IT BE?

A GENIUS.

I COULD BE IN A MAGAZINE WHEN THEY HAVE THEIR ISSUE FEATURING GENIUSES.

IT'D BE, LIKE, "THE FACE OF GENIUS TODAY."

AND THEN THERE'D BE A PICTURE OF ME.

WHAT DO YOU VALUE THE MOST IN OTHERS?
FRIENDSHIP.

NOTHING BETTER THAN SOMEONE WHO'S A TRUE FRIEND.

DO YOU PREFER BEING A ROBOT OR A VEHICLE?
KIND OF IN-BETWEEN...

LIKE A VEHICLE, BUT WITH MY HEAD STICKING OUT.

IS THAT WEIRD?

AN INTERVIEW WITH ARSONAL
WHAT ARE YOUR HOBBIES?
FILM, AND PHOTOGRAPHY.
I'M WORKING ON A NATURE DOCUMENTARY RIGHT NOW.
WHAT DOES CHANGE MEAN TO YOU?
THAT'S A GOOD QUESTION.
CHANGE IS ALL ABOUT GETTING BACK TO WHERE YOU STARTED.
I'M ALL ABOUT FIGHTING CHANGE.
WHAT ARE YOUR GOALS?
TO MAKE IT A YEAR WITHOUT BEING SHOT.
I'M AT SEVEN MONTHS, EIGHT DAYS RIGHT NOW.
INVINCIBILITY OR SUPER SPEED?
ARE YOU SERIOUS?
DO YOU KNOW HOW MANY TIMES I'VE BEEN DESTROYED?
INVINCIBILITY, DEFINITELY.

AN INTERVIEW WITH STINKY
DO YOU PREFER BEING A ROBOT OR VEHICLE?
ROBOT.
WHEN I'M A VEHICLE IT CAN BE UNCOMFORTABLE BECAUSE I HAVE TO PUT THIS PART..
ER, YEAH, ROBOT.
WHAT GOALS DO YOU HAVE?
I'D LIKE TO CLEAN UP THE WORLD.
BUT NOT SO MUCH THAT I'D NO LONGER BE USEFUL.
WHO IS YOUR FAVORITE CHANGE-BOT?
BIG RIG.
HE'S PRETTY GREAT.
IF YOU COULD BE ANYTHING, WHAT WOULD IT BE?
THAT'S A TOUGH ONE.
I WOULD BE...
A WRITER.
NO, WAIT -- A PRIVATE EYE.

AN INTERVIEW WITH RUSTY
WHAT DOES CHANGE MEAN TO YOU?
HUH?
IT MEANS THE DIFFERENCE BETWEEN A CURRENT STATE AND PREVIOUS STATE OF BEING.
WHAT'S IT SUPPOSED TO MEAN?
WHAT DO PEOPLE SEE IN YOU?
I DON'T KNOW, AND I DON'T CARE.
I'M MY OWN VAN.
INVISIBILITY OR FLIGHT?
NEITHER.
I DON'T NEED THAT KIND OF EXTRA RESPONSIBILITY.
WHAT ARE YOUR GOALS?
I'VE GOT ONE GOAL:
NEVER GIVE THEM THE SATISFACTION.
NEVER EVER.

AN INTERVIEW WITH AFTERBURNERBOT
IF YOU COULD BE ANYTHING, WHAT WOULD IT BE?
I WOULD BE WHOLE AGAIN.
WHAT DO PEOPLE SEE IN YOU?
THEY CRINGE.
THEY SEE WHAT THEIR WAR HAS DONE...
I GUESS I MAKE THEM UNCOMFORT-ABLE.
DO YOU PREFER BEING A ROBOT OR VEHICLE?
I'M JUST A HEAD.
VEHICLE, OBVIOUSLY.
INVISIBILITY OR FLIGHT?
I SEE WHAT YOU'RE TRYING TO DO.
IT'S NOT GOING TO WORK. I'M NOT GOING TO STOOP TO YOUR LEVEL.
JERK.

AN INTERVIEW WITH SHOOTERTRON
DO YOU HAVE ANY BAD HABITS?
YES.
TALKING TO INSUFFERABLE FOOLS.
WHAT DO PEOPLE SEE IN YOU?
FEAR.
NO, WAIT, THAT DOESN'T MAKE SENSE. IT WOULD MEAN I'M AFRAID...
THEY SEE... WHAT... THEY'RE AFRAID OF.
WHO IS YOUR FAVORITE CHANGE-BOT?
I LIKE THEM ALL.
JUST KIDDING.
IF YOU COULD BE ANYTHING, WHAT WOULD YOU BE?
A PIRATE.
WHAT?

AN INTERVIEW WITH BIG RIG
WHAT DO PEOPLE SEE IN YOU?
UM...
WHAT DO THEY SEE IN ME?
A LEADER. COURAGE. COMMITMENT. UM, VALUES. THEY SEE VALUES IN ME.
NOT JUST ANY VALUES, EITHER. TRADITIONAL VALUES. THE GOOD KIND.
WHAT DOES CHANGE MEAN TO YOU?
IT MEANS GETTING BETTER AND BETTER.
IMPROVING. EVOLVING.
WHAT ARE YOUR HOBBIES?
TRAINING.
I TRAIN HARD. PLAY HARD. DOING STUFF HARD.
INVISIBILITY OR FLIGHT?
FLIGHT.
MORE USEFUL. IF YOU NEED TO RETREAT FAST, OR-ER, NOT THAT I'D EVER RETREAT.

AN INTERVIEW WITH BALLS
DO YOU PREFER BEING A ROBOT OR A VEHICLE?
IT DEPENDS.
MOSTLY ROBOT.
IT MAKES ME FEEL MORE CONFIDENT.
DO YOU HAVE ANY BAD HABITS?
YEAH, BUT THEY CAN'T BE THAT BAD.
THEY HAVEN'T KILLED ME.
YET.
WHAT ARE YOUR HOBBIES?
SAME AS MY BAD HABITS.
PRETTY MUCH.
IF YOU COULD BE ANYTHING, WHAT WOULD IT BE?
HOLD ON, I'M STILL THINKING.

AN INTERVIEW WITH SPARKY
WHAT DOES CHANGE MEAN TO YOU?
IT MEANS A TRANSITION TO A STATE OF GREATER ENTROPY.
DON'T ASK ME WHAT ENTROPY MEANS, THOUGH.
HOW DO YOU RELAX?
I JUST CLIMB INTO A LITTLE BOX...
JUST CLIMB IN THERE AND SNUGGLE UP.
DO YOU BELIEVE IN A HIGHER POWER?
YES.
BUT NOT AN AFTERLIFE.
I BELIEVE IN A CRUEL HIGHER POWER.
INVISIBILITY OR FLIGHT?
INVISIBILITY.
EVERYONE STARTED PUTTING IN MOTION DETECTORS.
THEY'RE ON TO ME.

AN
INTERVIEW
WITH
OLD TIMEY

WHAT DOES CHANGE MEAN TO YOU?
LISTEN-

WHEN YOU'VE BEEN AROUND AS LONG AS I HAVE, YOU'LL KNOW, NOTHING CHANGES.

IT'S JUST ONE BIG NEVER ENDING SAME.

WHAT DO PEOPLE SEE IN YOU?

I'M SORRY, WHAT?

DO YOU PREFER BEING A ROBOT OR VEHICLE?
EITHER.

IT'S GOING BACK AND FORTH FROM ONE TO THE OTHER I DON'T CARE FOR.

CREAKKK

WHAT ARE YOUR GOALS?
GOALS?

TOO LATE FOR THAT.

AN INTERVIEW WITH MICROWAVE
WHAT DOES CHANGE MEAN TO YOU?
NOT MUCH.
SAME OLD, SAME OLD AS FAR AS I'M CONCERNED.
WHAT DO PEOPLE SEE IN YOU?
SOUPY AND POPPER.
IF THOSE TWO KNOW WHAT'S GOOD FOR THEM!
DO YOU HAVE ANY BAD HABITS?
I WISH!
I MEAN, I'VE GOT TWO LITTLE ONES TO TAKE CARE OF.
THEY WATCH ME, LEARN FROM ME...
I CAN ONLY IMAGINE HOW ANNOYING THEY'D BE IF THEY HAD MY BAD HABITS.
INVINCIBILITY OR SUPER SPEED?
THAT'S EASY, INVINCIBILITY.
UNLESS IT'S, LIKE, INFINITELY FAST SUPER SPEED.
BECAUSE THEN YOU COULD JUST AVOID ALL DANGER.

AN INTERVIEW WITH EJECT
WHAT DOES CHANGE MEAN TO YOU?
OOH!
INCREDIBLE CHANGE!
CHEE
CHOO
CHEE
CHOOK
SEE HOW I DID THAT?
WHAT DO PEOPLE SEE IN YOU?
THEY SEE LEADERSHIP.
THEY SEE HONOR. THEY SEE FAIR AND BAL---OH.
WERE YOU SETTING ME UP FOR THAT ONE? MISSED IT. SORRY.
INVISIBILITY OR FLIGHT?
INVISIBILITY.
IT'S USEFUL AND FUN.
HOW DO YOU RELAX?
NO ONE SAYS "RELAX" ANYMORE.
I DON'T RELAX. I CHILL.

AN INTERVIEW WITH WHEEEEE
DO YOU PREFER BEING A ROBOT OR VEHICLE?
I'M HAPPY EITHER WAY...
WHICH DO YOU PREFER ME TO BE?
WHAT ARE YOUR HOBBIES?
OH, GEEZ..
REALLY, I DON'T HAVE TIME FOR HOBBIES.
I BELIEVE IN HARD WORK, DEDICATION AND BEING COMPETITIVE.
INVINCIBILITY OR SUPER SPEED?
INVINCIBILITY.
AS YOU KNOW, I ALREADY HAVE SUPER SPEED.
IF YOU COULD BE ANYTHING, WHAT WOULD YOU BE?
IN CHARGE.
AND I CAN BE.
I CAN BE ANYTHING I WANT IF I PUT MY MIND TO IT.
ONCE ANY OBSTACLES ARE...REMOVED.

AN INTERVIEW WITH HOSER
IF YOU COULD BE ANYTHING, WHAT WOULD IT BE?
SAME AS EVERYONE:
ROCK STAR.
DO YOU HAVE ANY BAD HABITS?
I'M ALWAYS LATE.
ALTHOUGH, THAT'S NOT REALLY A HABIT, IS IT?
WELL I GUESS IF I "MAKE A HABIT" OF BEING LATE.
I DON'T THINK THAT'S REALLY WHAT THIS QUESTION WAS ABOUT, THOUGH.
WHAT DO YOU MOST VALUE IN OTHERS?
LIKE, ONE THING?
BECAUSE I LIKE TO JUDGE OTHERS ON A CASE BY CASE BASIS.
TELEKINESIS OR TELEPATHY?
WELL, TELEPATHY WOULD BE MORE USEFUL.
BUT THEN IT ALSO HAS MORE OF A DOWNSIDE TOO.
SO... NO, I'LL GO WITH TELEPATHY.

AN INTERVIEW WITH IVY
WHAT ARE YOUR GOALS?
I'D LIKE TO CURE SOMETHING.
I DON'T KNOW WHAT THOUGH.
JUST NOT SOMETHING STUPID.
WHAT DO PEOPLE SEE IN YOU?
I'M VERY KIND.
EASY TO GET ALONG WITH.
GOOD IN THE GARAGE.
WHO'S YOUR FAVORITE CHANGE-BOT?
HONKYTONK.
ER, DON'T TELL SIREN.
IF YOU COULD BE ANYTHING, WHAT WOULD IT BE?
SOME KIND OF AMPHIBIOUS VEHICLE...
THAT COULD GO ON LAND, BUT THEN GO UNDER WATER TOO.
IS THERE SOMETHING LIKE THAT?

AN INTERVIEW WITH HONKYTONK AND SIREN
WHAT ARE YOUR GOALS?
I THINK TO HAVE A FAMILY.
WELL, I MEAN, WE ARE A FAMILY ALREADY, REALLY.
WELL, YEAH, I THINK OF YOU AS MY FAMILY, BUT...
YOU KNOW...
INVISIBILITY OR FLIGHT?
INVISIBILITY.
FLIGHT.
DO YOU PREFER BEING ROBOTS OR VEHICLES?
ROBOTS.
IF YOU COULD BE ANYTHING, WHAT WOULD IT BE?
TOGETHER.
FOREVER.
BLARRRGGHHK!
WHAT'S THAT NOISE?

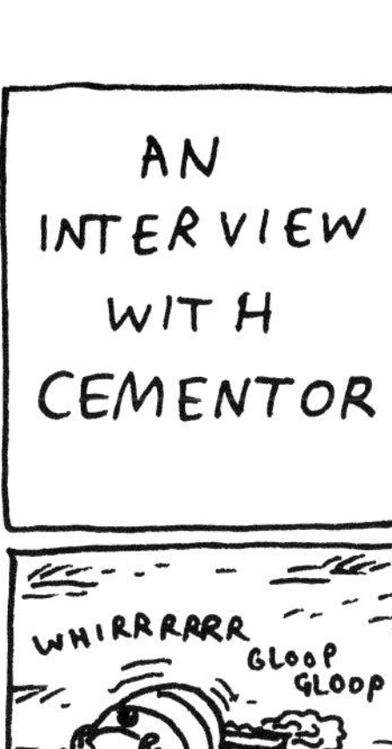
AN INTERVIEW WITH CEMENTOR

WHAT DOES CHANGE MEAN TO YOU?
TO ME, CHANGE IS ALL ABOUT--

OH, HOLD ON A SEC.

WHIRRRRRRR
GLOOP GLOOP

WHIRRRRRRR
GLOOP GLOOP
GLOOP

AH. OKAY, WHAT WERE WE TALKING ABOUT?

WHAT ARE YOUR HOBBIES?
BUILDING FORTS.

BUT, YOU KNOW, ACTUAL FORTS.

DO YOU PREFER BEING A ROBOT OR VEHICLE?
IT USED TO BE ROBOT...

THESE DAYS IT'S VEHICLE. IT'S EASIER ON MY BACK.

WHO IS YOUR LEAST FAVORITE CHANGE-BOT?
RACEY.

HE'S TOO COCKY. I'D LIKE TO KNOCK HIM DOWN A PEG.

AN
INTERVIEW
WITH
BUSHWACKY

DO YOU PREFER BEING A ROBOT OR A VEHICLE?
ROBOT.

I CAN HOLD TWO GUNS AT A TIME THAT WAY.

WHAT ARE YOUR GOALS?
TO BE THE BEST THERE IS.

BE ABLE TO SHOOT MORE, STUFF MORE OFTEN.

101% SHOOTING ACCURACY.

HOLD AN EXTRA GUN IN MY MOUTH TO SHOOT STUFF.

BE A SHOOTING MACHINE.

I'M ALREADY A SHOOTING MACHINE, BUT YOU KNOW WHAT I MEAN.

INVISIBILITY OR FLIGHT?
INVISIBILITY.

I'M PRETTY SURE I COULD ALREADY FLY IF I WANTED.

WHO'S YOUR FAVORITE CHANGE-BOT?
ME.

AN INTERVIEW WITH GASSER

WHAT'S YOUR FAVORITE MOVIE GENRE?
I DON'T WATCH MOVIES.

THOSE THINGS WILL ROT YOUR MIND.

I PREFER TO JUST DOWNLOAD DIGITAL VISUAL INFORMATION RIGHT INTO MY HEAD.

DO YOU HAVE ANY GOALS?
YES.

OH! YES, I WOULD LIKE TO OWN MY OWN BUSINESS.

WHAT ARE YOUR HOBBIES?
SPORTS FAN. I'M A BIG SPORTS FAN.

HELPS ME HOLD BACK THE DARKNESS JUST A LITTLE BIT.

INVINCIBILITY OR SUPER SPEED?
SUPER SPEED.

I CAN'T IMAGINE INVINCIBILITY IS ANYTHING BUT BORING.

AN INTERVIEW WITH JITTERS
WHAT ARE YOUR HOBBIES?
SCRAPBOOKING.
I DON'T REALLY MAKE ANY SCRAPBOOKS, THOUGH.
I JUST LIKE ALL THE MATERIALS.
HOW DO YOU RELAX?
I JUST GO OUT AND GET AWAY...
HAVE NO ONE ELSE AROUND, SPEND SOME TIME BY MYSELF.
AAAAAHHHH.
WHAT DO YOU VALUE THE MOST IN OTHERS?
STRENGTH.
I DON'T NEED SOMEONE TELLING ME WHAT TO DO,
BUT I DON'T MIND IT.
TELEKINESIS OR TELEPATHY?
TELEKINESIS.
THEN YOU COULD DO ONE THING BUT THEN DO ANOTHER WITH YOUR MIND AT THE SAME TIME.
THEY SAY IT WOULDN'T WORK THAT WAY BUT I'LL BET ITS LIKE WALKING AND CHEWING GUM.

AN INTERVIEW WITH DOZER
DO YOU PREFER BEING A ROBOT OR VEHICLE?
THAT'S A STUPID QUESTION.
IT DEPENDS, OBVIOUSLY.
WHAT ARE YOUR HOBBIES?
ARMCHAIR PHILOSOPHY.
LANDSCAPING.
COLLECTING STUFF.
TELEKINESIS OR TELEPATHY?
TELEPATHY.
YOU COULD USE IT AND NO ONE WOULD EVER KNOW.
BOTH ARE IMPOSSIBLE, OF COURSE.
IF YOU COULD BE ANYTHING, WHAT WOULD IT BE?
A REAL PHILOSOPHER.
I JUST DON'T HAVE THE TIME.
I'D BE TOTALLY A GREAT PHILOSOPHER IF I HAD THE TIME.

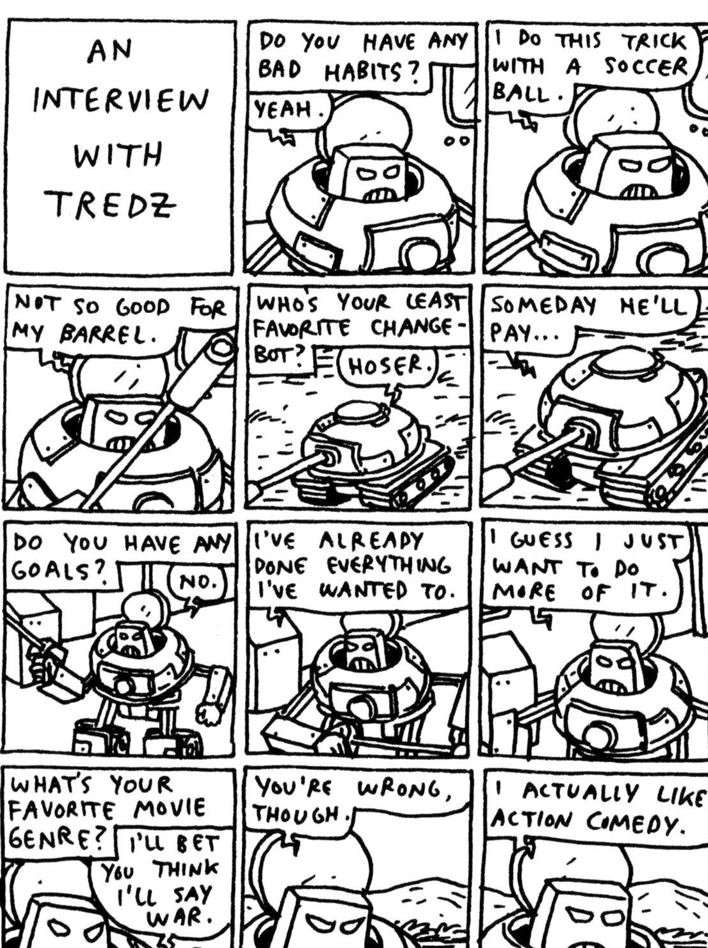
AN INTERVIEW WITH TREDZ
DO YOU HAVE ANY BAD HABITS?
YEAH.
I DO THIS TRICK WITH A SOCCER BALL.
NOT SO GOOD FOR MY BARREL.
WHO'S YOUR LEAST FAVORITE CHANGE-BOT?
HOSER.
SOMEDAY HE'LL PAY...
DO YOU HAVE ANY GOALS?
NO.
I'VE ALREADY DONE EVERYTHING I'VE WANTED TO.
I GUESS I JUST WANT TO DO MORE OF IT.
WHAT'S YOUR FAVORITE MOVIE GENRE?
I'LL BET YOU THINK I'LL SAY WAR.
YOU'RE WRONG, THOUGH.
I ACTUALLY LIKE ACTION COMEDY.

AN INTERVIEW WITH RACEY
WHAT DO PEOPLE SEE IN YOU?
PEOPLE LIKE ME.
I'M NOT ALL FLASH AND DASH, I'M ALSO DOWN TO EARTH.
I THINK THEY LIKE WHAT THEY SEE, THOUGH.
DO YOU HAVE ANY BAD HABITS?
NOT REALLY.
NEED TO KEEP IT CLEAN TO HAVE THE KIND OF PERFORMANCE I WANT TO HAVE.
INVISIBILITY OR FLIGHT?
NEITHER.
YOU ALREADY WON'T SEE ME COMING.
DO YOU BELIEVE IN A HIGHER POWER?
DON'T REALLY THINK ABOUT IT.
IF THERE IS, THERE IS, IF THERE ISN'T, THERE ISN'T.
DOESN'T REALLY MAKE A PRACTICAL DIFFERENCE TO ME.
EEEEEEEEEEE

AN INTERVIEW WITH STEGGY AND BUZZY
WHAT DO YOU VALUE THE MOST IN OTHERS?
SOMEONE WHO TAKES CARE OF YOU.
BUT ALSO TRUSTS YOU ON YOUR OWN.
YEAH. BUT THEY PROVIDE YOU WITH A LOT OF COMFORT.
RIGHT. BUT NOT LIKE, THEY'RE CO-DEPENDENT OR SOMETHING.
TELEKINESIS OR TELEPATHY?
TELEPATHY.
BOTH.
OH, YEAH, THAT'S A GOOD IDEA. I WANT BOTH TOO.
DO YOU HAVE ANY BAD HABITS?
I CHEW ON MY WINGS SOMETIMES.
I CHEW ON HIS WINGS TOO.
WHAT'S YOUR FAVORITE MOVIE GENRE?
COMEDY.
HISTORICAL DOCU-DRAMA.

AN INTERVIEW WITH SOUPY AND POPPER
INVINCIBILITY OR SUPER SPEED?
INVINCIBILITY.
SUPER SPEED.
IF YOU COULD BE ANYTHING, WHAT WOULD IT BE?
IDENTIFIED AS AN INDIVIDUAL.
A TRUCK.
WHAT DO OTHERS SEE IN YOU?
WELL...
I FEEL LIKE PEOPLE DON'T TAKE US SERIOUSLY BECAUSE OF OUR SIZE.
AND BECAUSE WE GOOF AROUND.
BUT MOSTLY OUR SIZE.
WHAT ARE YOUR HOBBIES?
I WANT TO GO HOME.
CAN WE GO HOME NOW?

AN
INTERVIEW
WITH
SHADOW XGX-9

HOW DO YOU RELAX?
DRIVING.

I LIKE TO GET OUT ON THE ROAD, REALLY OPEN IT UP.

REALLY PUSH THE LIMITS OF SPEED.

ACTUALLY THAT'S NOT REALLY VERY RELAXING.

IT'S MORE A WAY OF BURNING OFF STEAM.

KIND OF GETS ME RILED UP, ACTUALLY.

WHAT DOES CHANGE MEAN TO YOU?
IT MEANS NEVER HAVING TO SAY YOU'RE SORRY.

BUT THEN LATER YOU HAVE TO SAY YOU'RE SORRY.

DO YOU BELIEVE IN A HIGHER POWER?
YES.

BUT NOT AN INTELLIGENT HIGHER POWER.

INVISIBILITY OR FLIGHT?
FLIGHT. I'M ALREADY INVISIBLE.

WHAT?!
ALL RIGHT, THAT'S IT! THIS INTERVIEW IS OVER!
STORM
KLANG
CLANG

AN INCREDIBLE CHANGE-BOTS FREE COMIC BOOK DAY STORY

IN THE AFTERMATH OF THEIR MOST RECENT CLIMACTIC BATTLE, THE CHANGE-BOTS ARE TRYING TO LEARN ABOUT EARTH CULTURE IN ORDER TO BETTER FIT IN...
AND THAT ENDS OUR REPORT ON REALITY TELEVISION.
THANK YOU, MICROWAVE. NEXT UP IS BIG RIG, REPORTING ON COMIC BOOKS.
THANKS, SHOOTY. COMIC BOOKS ARE A HIGHLY COLLECTIBLE ENTER-TAINMENT PRODUCT.
I'VE BROUGHT SOME SAMPLES. AS YOU CAN SEE, THEY COVER A NUMBER OF GENRES, NONE OF WHICH ARE FOR KIDS.
YES, EJECT?
WHY ARE THEY IN BAGS?

THESE BAGS PROTECT THE COMIC BOOKS, INCREASING THEIR VALUE.
I'VE ARRANGED FOR US TO TAKE A FIELD TRIP TO AN ACTUAL COMIC BOOK SHOP.
THIS SATURDAY IS FREE COMIC BOOK DAY!
WE CAN ALL GO AND GET FREE COMICS, WHICH CAN ONLY INCREASE IN VALUE!
UH, BECAUSE THEY'RE FREE...?
SOON, WE WILL HAVE UNTOLD AMOUNTS OF EARTH WEALTH...

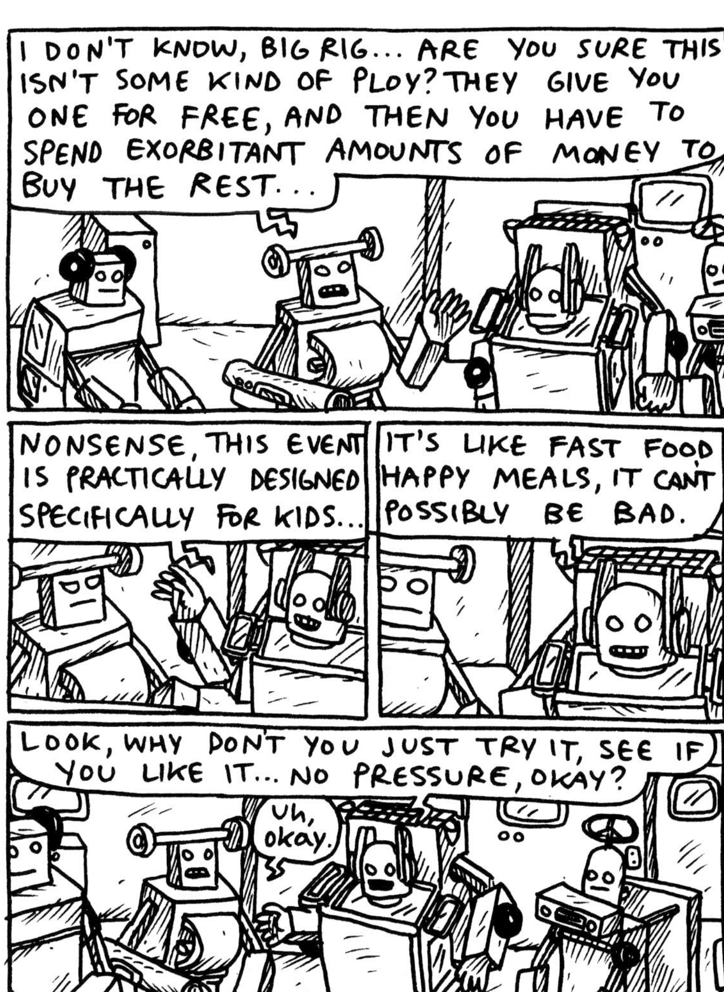
I DON'T KNOW, BIG RIG... ARE YOU SURE THIS ISN'T SOME KIND OF PLOY? THEY GIVE YOU ONE FOR FREE, AND THEN YOU HAVE TO SPEND EXORBITANT AMOUNTS OF MONEY TO BUY THE REST...
NONSENSE, THIS EVENT IS PRACTICALLY DESIGNED SPECIFICALLY FOR KIDS...
IT'S LIKE FAST FOOD HAPPY MEALS, IT CAN'T POSSIBLY BE BAD.
LOOK, WHY DON'T YOU JUST TRY IT, SEE IF YOU LIKE IT... NO PRESSURE, OKAY?
Uh, okay.

SATURDAY!
OOH!
TP SNAP
INCREDIBLE CHANGE!
CHEE CHOO CHE CHOOK
CHEE
I GUESS I SHOULD'VE INCREDIBLE-CHANGED BEFORE I CAME IN..

HEY, WHAT ARE YOU GUYS DOING IN HERE?!
STOP THAT!
DO YOU HAVE X-MEN #192?
OOPS
OOPS
So, RUSTY, THESE ARE ALL FREE?
RIPPPPPPPP
UH, YEAH, I GUESS SO..
HUH

I'M GOING TO GET THIS WHOLE RUN OF MILLER/ MAZZUCCHELLI DAREDEVIL.
YOU SHOULD FOCUS ON NUMBER ONES, THOSE ARE ALWAYS WORTH MORE. AND VARIANT REPRINT COVERS...
CRASH!
SORRY!
STOP!! GET OUT OF MY SHOP!
OKAY, GEEZ!

THIS WAS THE SCENE YESTERDAY AS FREE COMIC BOOK DAY TURNED INTO CHAOS...
WHEN MARAUDING CHANGE-BOTS TRASHED THE LOCAL COMIC SHOP!
I DON'T KNOW WHY, THEY JUST REALLY WENT AFTER 1980'S LIMITED SERIES AND CROSSOVERS.
I'D SAY MY LOSSES ARE IN THE HUNDREDS OF DOLLARS.
...BUT THE REAL LOSS IS THESE IRREPLACEABLE CULTURAL ARTIFACTS. WHEN WILL THE TERROR END?
COMIX

WELL, I GUESS WE CAN AGREE THAT WAS A TOTAL FAILURE.
NOT AT ALL! I GOT THIS CGC 7.8 UNCANNY X-MEN #142!
YES, BUT AT WHAT COST?
IT WAS FREE!
NO, I MEAN THE IMMEASURABLE COST... ONCE AGAIN, WE'VE BEGUN TO LOSE THE TRUST AND RESPECT OF THE HUMANS!

CLEARLY, WE MISUNDERSTOOD THE NATURE OF THIS EVENT. I THINK WHAT WE WERE SUPPOSED TO DO IS FREE THE COMIC BOOKS!
HUMANS VALUE FREEDOM. WE WILL REGAIN THEIR RESPECT BY GIVING FREEDOM TO THEIR PRECIOUS COMIC BOOKS!
HOW WOULD WE DO THAT?
WHAT ABOUT A CAMPAIGN OF IMPASSIONED LETTER WRITING?
NO, WHAT WE NEED IS ACTION! WE'LL CONDUCT A SECRET, COVERT NIGHT OPERATION TO FREE THE COMICS.
ONCE THE COMIC BOOKS ARE FREE, WE'LL BE PRAISED AS HEROES!

SO IF THIS MISSION IS SECRET, HOW WILL THE HUMANS KNOW WE'RE RESPONSIBLE?
SHHHHH!

BIG RIG, WHY IS THE COMIC SHOP STILL OPEN?
I DON'T KNOW, IT SHOULD BE CLOSED BY NOW.

WAIT, I SEE... IT LOOKS LIKE THEY'RE HAVING A HEROCLIX TOURNAMENT.

WELL, WE CAN'T WAIT HERE ALL NIGHT...
INCREDIBLE CHANGE-BOTS... GO!

INCREDIBLE CHANGE!
CHEE
CHOO
CHEE
CHOOK
CHE
CHEE
CHOO
CHO
CHOOK

COMIC BOOKS!
Dangit, I was winning!
FREE THE COMIC BOOKS!
SPREAD OUT! FIND THE COMICS!
BIG RIG, LOOK! LONG BOXES!
THOSE ARE JUST THE QUARTER BINS. FIND THE SILVER AGE BACK ISSUES!

WHAT ABOUT THESE REALLY THICK COMIC BOOKS?
NO, THOSE ARE JUST TRADE PAPERBACK COLLECTIONS...
WHAT ABOUT THESE SHELVES MARKED "GRAPHIC NOVELS?"
GRAPHIC NOVELS
DEFINITELY NOT THOSE.
EVEN IF THEY WERE ORIGINALLY SERIALIZED?
GRAPHIC NOVELS
FROM
MICROWAVE! THOSE ARE JUST SELF-PUBLISHED ZINES AND MINICOMICS, IGNORE THEM!
BUT... THEY'RE COOL..
C'MON, EVERYONE! GO, GO, GO, GO!

WE'VE GOT THEM, NOW WHAT?
REMOVE THEM FROM THEIR MYLAR SLEEVES AND POLY-BAGS.
SHOOTERTRON, NO! WHAT ARE YOU DOING? THIS WASN'T PART OF THE PLAN!
NONSENSE, BIG RIG...
THIS WAS ALWAYS THE PLAN!
GASP!
NOOOOOOOOOO!
CAREFUL WITH THE TAPE ON BACK!

GOOD JOB, EVERYONE. LET'S GO!
YEAH!
ALRIGHT!
POKE
POKE
I'M SORRY.
Heh
NEXT: FREE WEBCOMIC DAY!

IN A WORLD FULL OF INCREDIBLE CHANGE-BOTS, NOT EVERYTHING IS WHAT IT FIRST APPEARS TO BE...

INCREDIBLE CHANGE-BOTS TWO!

JUST AS GOOD AS THE FIRST ONE! THE CHANGE-BOTS RETURN TO EARTH WITH MORE ROBOTS[1], MORE SHOOTING[2], MORE ACTION[3] AND MORE "FUNNY PARTS!"[4]

1 Really it's mostly the same robots, but some of them are drawn differently.

2 There's actually probably less shooting, but I haven't counted, so I can't say for sure.

3 Er, define "action."

4 I guess instead of more I should really say "as much" and "as many." Sorry.

NO, NO, IT'S OKAY. I'VE GOT LOTS TO DO TONIGHT ANYWAY...
YEAH. HEH HEH. OKAY... SEE YOU SOON.
HEY BALLS, ARE YOU OKAY? YOU'RE LOOKING A LITTLE-
DON'T SAY IT. DON'T SAY IT!
BEW!
BEW!
BEW!
BEW!
"DOWN"! I WAS GOING TO SAY "DOWN"!
NEXT: WHAT COMES AFTER THE BLUES!

BIGHEAD SUPER TEAM-UP
FEATURING
INCREDIBLE CHANGE-BOTS!
I'M A JET!
INCREDIBLE CHANGE!
CHOO-CHUH-CHICK-CHOO-CHA!
I AM A ROBOT!
BEWWWW!
NOW I'M A ROBOT!
INCREDIBLE CHANGE!
CHEE-CHOO-CHOCK-CHO-CHEW!
BEEYEWW!
HOW CAN MAN FACE MACHINERY WHICH FEELS NO EMOTION?!
NOW I'M A CAR WITH A GUN ON IT!

THE TEST
A SHOOTERTRON SHORT

SO, THE FIRST QUESTION OF THIS PERSONALITY TEST IS: WHAT ARE YOUR STRENGTHS?
HM... 7.

NO, WAIT! 9.
ER, AND WHAT ARE YOUR WEAKNESSES?

WEAKNESS? EXCUSE ME?
ER, WHAT ARE YOUR... GOOD QUALITIES, IN CONTRAST TO YOUR GREAT QUALITIES?

HM. CAN'T THINK OF ANY. WELL, ACTUALLY.. NOPE. THEY'RE ALL GREAT.

IF YOU COULD CHANGE ONE THING ABOUT YOURSELF, WHAT WOULD IT BE?

A BIG GUN!
A BIG GUN?

I WOULD CHANGE INTO A BIG, HUGE GUN. THAT WOULD BE PRETTY COOL.

WAIT A MINUTE, IS THIS SOME KIND OF TEST?
YES, A PERSONALITY TEST. I SAID THAT.

HA HA! WELL PLAYED, WELL PLAYED. TRY AND TEST ME, THEN. JUST TRY AND TEST ME!

ER, THAT'S ALL FOR TODAY, ACTUALLY.

HOW DID I DO?
YOU DID GREAT.

AN INCREDIBLE CHANGE-BOTS CHRISTMAS!
HERE YOU GO, BIG RIG.

YOU GOT ME A PRESENT? THANKS!

INCREDIBLE CHANGE!
CHEE CHOO
CHEE CHOOK

A VIDEO CHANGE-BOT!
HOW YOU DOIN'?

DID I DO THAT?

UH...
I KNOW NOTHINK!
YEAH. IT ONLY TALKS IN SITCOM CATCHPHRASES.

WHACHOO TALKIN' ABOUT?

WELL, EXCUUUUUSE ME!

WOULD YOU BE OFFENDED IF I SHOT IT?
HOW RUDE!
IT IS HIGH DEFINITION, YOU KNOW.

INCREDIBLE CHANGE-UP #1

OUCH.

DOZER AND TREDZ:
DEEP CONVERSATIONS

HEY TREDZ, DO YOU EVER THINK ABOUT THE BIGGER THINGS IN LIFE?

YOU MEAN, LIKE, MOUNTAINS AND STUFF?

NO, I MEAN THE REALLY BIG--
PLANETS?
NO, LIKE--
BLACK HOLES? GALAXIES?

NO, NO, LET ME TALK. I MEAN THE BIG QUESTIONS...

LIKE, WILL THERE EVER BE AN END TO WAR AND SUFFERING?

WHAT DOES IT MEAN TO BE ALIVE? ARE WE ALL DOOMED TO LIVE ALONE IN OUR OWN MINDS?

CAN LOVE EXIST BEYOND THE END OF AN INDIVIDUAL CONSCIOUSNESS?

WILL THE HEAT DEATH OF THE UNIVERSE LAST FOREVER?

MOSTLY I JUST THINK ABOUT SHOOTING STUFF.

YEAH, WE ALL THINK ABOUT SHOOTING STUFF, SURE, BUT YOU NEVER THINK ABOUT WHAT LIFE MEANS?
NOT REALLY.

BEW! BEW! BEW!

SHOOTING STUFF IS SWEET!
IS IT EVER THE END?

Jeffrey Brown

Jeffrey Brown

BALLS ON PATROL

BEW!
BEW!

SOUPY! POPPER! FLANKING ATTACK!
OH WAIT, I FORGOT MY GUN

THERE'S TOO MANY! I'LL JUST SHOOT THE SMALLER ONES SO IT LOOKS LIKE I PUT UP MORE OF A FIGHT.
BEW! BEW!

GRAB HIM!
OKAY, OKAY I GIVE UP!

TAKE HIM BACK TO THE MEGACAVE... HE'LL PAY FOR THIS!

NOW THAT WE'VE GOT BALLS, WE CAN FINALLY DEFEAT THE AWESOMEBOTS!

ALLOW ME TO INTERROGATE THE PRISONER, SHOOTERTRON. ONE MINUTE IN MY BELLY ON DEFROST AND HE'LL TELL US THE AWESOMEBOT PLAN!

WAIT? WHAT'S THIS?
SHINY!

DEFIANTLY, BALLS STRUGGLES AGAINST HIS CAPTORS
I'LL NEVER TALK! NEVER!
BUT YOU'RE TALKING RIGHT NOW.

WHAT IS IT?
A SHINY BLINKING LIGHT CAN ONLY BE ONE THING: A HOMING BEACON!

THAT'S RIGHT! YOU'VE GOT BALLS? I AM BALLS!

AWESOMEBOTS-SURPRISSSSE!
I MEAN, SURPRISE ATTACKKKK!
BEW!
BDEW!

THE AWESOMEBOTS TAKE THE FANTASTICONS BY COMPLETE SURPRISE...
WOO HOO!
KLANG!
OOH! I'M COMPLETELY SURPRISED!

QUICKLY, THE AWESOMEBOTS AND FANTASTICONS ARE EMBROILED IN A FIERCE BATTLE...
HEY, GET OFF MY HOOD!
BEW!
BDEW!

BEW!
AUGGHHH!
BDEW!

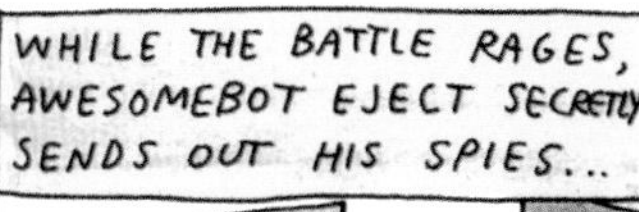
WHILE THE BATTLE RAGES, AWESOMEBOT EJECT SECRETLY SENDS OUT HIS SPIES...

NGHHH

FREEZE! WHAT ARE YOU AWESOMEBOTS DOING BACK HERE?
UM, NOTHING?

WELL, I GUESS YOU'RE PRETTY HARMLESS, BEING OUTDATED TECHNOLOGY AND ALL... MOVE ALONG.
YEAH, WE'RE JUST CASSETTE TAPES.
YEAH, LET US GO.

AFTER ALMOST GETTING CAUGHT, THE AWESOMEBOTS QUICKLY RETURN TO THEIR SECRET MISSION...
DID YOU FIND IT?
NO.

HEY! WHAT ARE YOU DOING HERE?!
BEW!
RUN!
UGH! SAVE YOURSELF!

MEANWHILE, THE BATTLE CONTINUES TO RAGE...
HOW LONG ARE WE SUPPOSED TO FIGHT?
BEW!
UNTIL THE FANTASTICONS ARE CRUSHED FOREVER!
BEW!
NO, I MEAN IN THIS BATTLE.
OH. LIKE TEN MINUTES.
BEW!
BEW
BEW!

WAIT? WHO HAVEN'T I SHOT AT YET?
BEW!
BDEW!

SUDDENLY, AS QUICKLY AS THEY APPEARED, THE AWESOMEBOTS LEAVE!
AWESOMEBOTS, GO!
NO, THE OTHER WAY!
OH

LOOK, THEY'RE RETREATING!
NO WE'RE NOT, WE'RE MAKING A TACTICAL WITHDRAWL.
BEW!
BDEW!

YEAH, WE WON!
AW MAN, I GOT HERE TOO LATE... I DIDN'T GET TO SHOOT ANYONE.
DUDE, IT WAS AWESOME.

LATER
HEY! SOMEBODY WAS IN MY ROOM!

OKAY, WHO WENT THROUGH MY DRAWERS?!
WHAT ARE YOU TALKING ABOUT?
GIVE IT BACK!
WHY ARE YOU ALL WACKED OUT?

HOW DARE YOU QUESTION ME?! I'LL SHOOT YOU ALL... ALLLLLLLLL!
RAZOW!

MEANWHILE, THE AWESOMEBOTS GATHER AROUND THEIR PRIZE.
GOOD JOB, EJECT! BUT WHAT IS THIS DEVICE?
IT'S CALLED A "POWER STRIP."... AND ONCE WE UNLOCK ITS SECRETS OUR ENERGY PROBLEMS WILL BE SOLVED!

BallsPa

BALLS PATROL

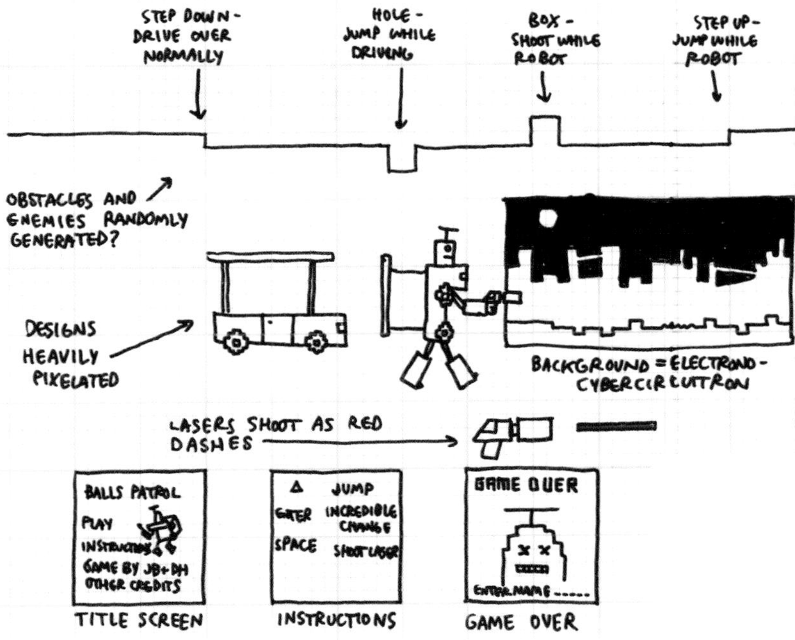
STEP DOWN - DRIVE OVER NORMALLY
HOLE - JUMP WHILE DRIVING
BOX - SHOOT WHILE ROBOT
STEP UP - JUMP WHILE ROBOT
OBSTACLES AND ENEMIES RANDOMLY GENERATED?
DESIGNS HEAVILY PIXELATED
BACKGROUND = ELECTRONO-CYBERCIRCUITRON
LASERS SHOOT AS RED DASHES
BALLS PATROL
PLAY
INSTRUCTIONS
GAME BY JB + DH
OTHER CREDITS
TITLE SCREEN
Δ JUMP
ENTER INCREDIBLE CHANGE
SPACE SHOOT LASER
INSTRUCTIONS
GAME OVER
ENTER NAME -----
GAME OVER

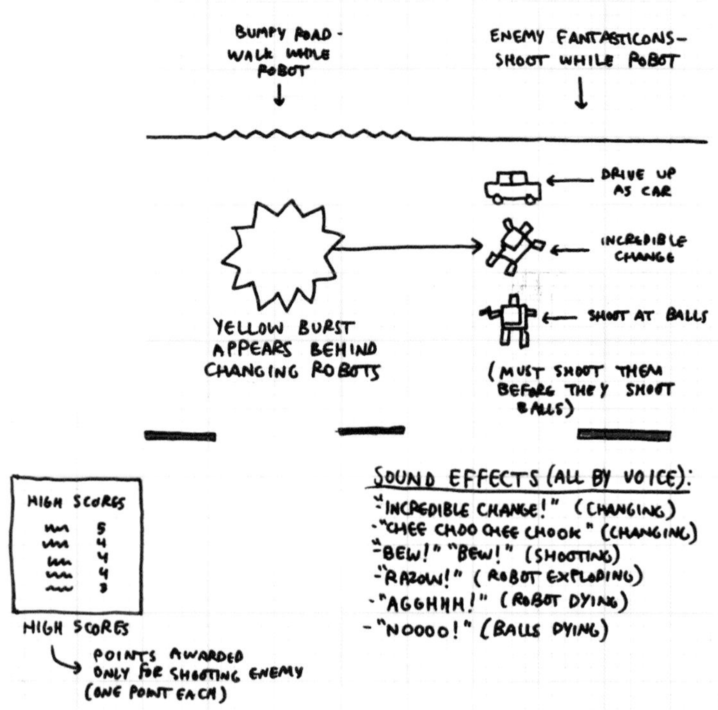
BUMPY ROAD - WALK WHILE ROBOT
ENEMY FANTASTICONS - SHOOT WHILE ROBOT
DRIVE UP AS CAR
INCREDIBLE CHANGE
SHOOT AT BALLS
YELLOW BURST APPEARS BEHIND CHANGING ROBOTS
(MUST SHOOT THEM BEFORE THEY SHOOT BALLS)
HIGH SCORES
5
4
4
4
3
HIGH SCORES
POINTS AWARDED ONLY FOR SHOOTING ENEMY (ONE POINT EACH)
SOUND EFFECTS (ALL BY VOICE):
-"INCREDIBLE CHANGE!" (CHANGING)
-"CHEE CHOO CHEE CHOOK" (CHANGING)
-"BEW!" "BEW!" (SHOOTING)
-"RAZOW!" (ROBOT EXPLODING)
-"AGGHHH!" (ROBOT DYING)
-"NOOOO!" (BALLS DYING)

UNLOCK SECRET BONUS CHARACTER: MICROWAVE

HOLD DOWN KEY WHILE ENTERING PLAY ON TITLE SCREEN (OR OTHER CODE?)

- DEFAULT MODE IS ROBOT FORM
- CHANGES INTO MICROWAVE, WHICH ONLY SITS THERE
- FIRE BUTTON CAUSES SOUPY AND POPPER TO COME OUT, AND JUST RUN AROUND (CANNOT CONTROL THEM)

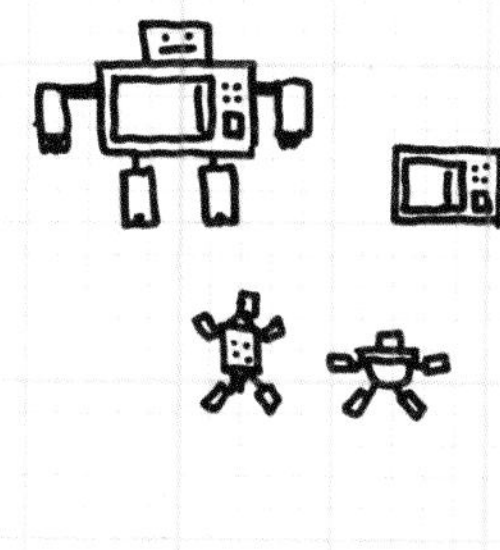

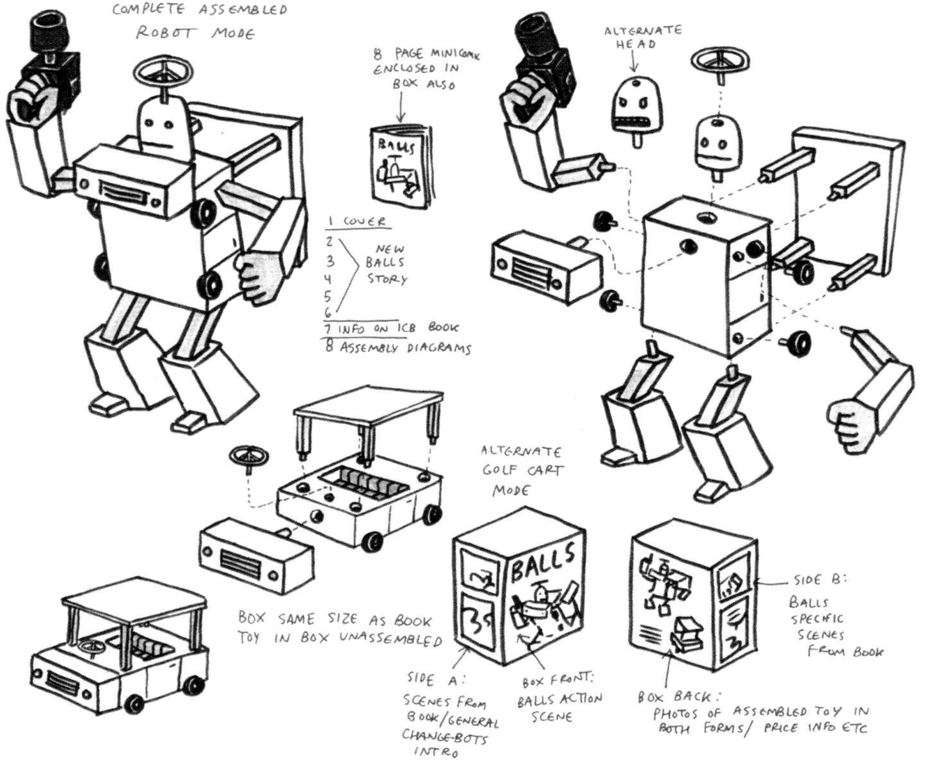
COMPLETE ASSEMBLED
ROBOT MODE
8 PAGE MINICOMIC
ENCLOSED IN
BOX ALSO
BALLS
1 COVER
2
3
4
5
6
NEW
BALLS
STORY
7 INFO ON ICB BOOK
8 ASSEMBLY DIAGRAMS
ALTERNATE
HEAD
ALTERNATE
GOLF CART
MODE
BOX SAME SIZE AS BOOK
TOY IN BOX UNASSEMBLED
BALLS
SIDE A:
SCENES FROM
BOOK/GENERAL
CHANGE-BOTS
INTRO
BOX FRONT:
BALLS ACTION
SCENE
BOX BACK:
PHOTOS OF ASSEMBLED TOY IN
BOTH FORMS/ PRICE INFO ETC
SIDE B:
BALLS
SPECIFIC
SCENES
FROM BOOK

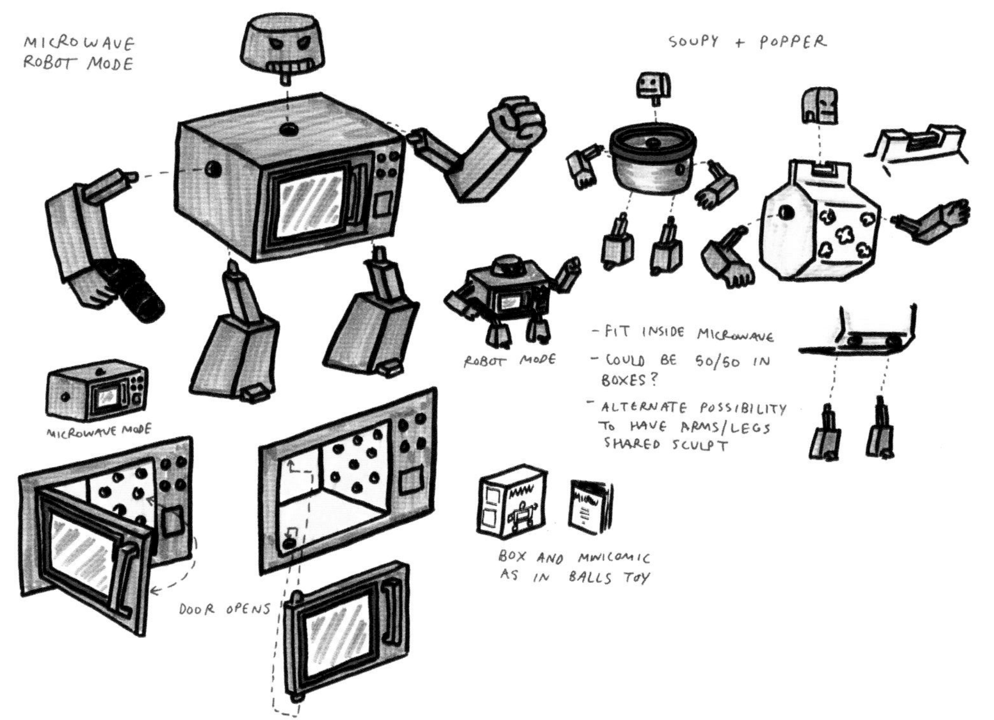
MICROWAVE
ROBOT MODE
SOUPY + POPPER
ROBOT MODE
- FIT INSIDE MICROWAVE
- COULD BE 50/50 IN
BOXES?
- ALTERNATE POSSIBILITY
TO HAVE ARMS/LEGS
SHARED SCULPT
MICROWAVE MODE
DOOR OPENS
BOX AND MINICOMIC
AS IN BALLS TOY

POP

FINAL PRODUCT MAY VARY

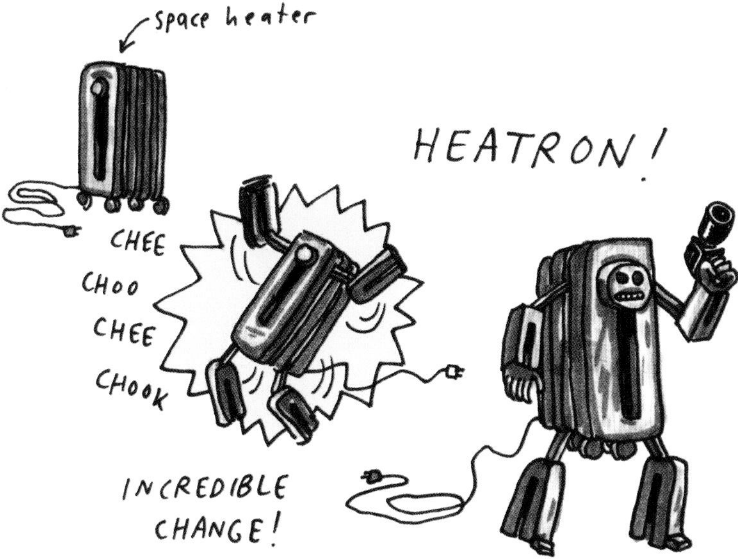

space heater

HEATRON!

CHEE
CHOO
CHEE
CHOOK

INCREDIBLE
CHANGE!

PENDLETON WARD, VICE-PRESIDENT OF THE INCREDIBLE CHANGE-BOTS FAN CLUB, SHOWS OFF HIS LOVE OF BALLS WITH THIS SWEET FAN ART!

You should make Change-Bot Underoos.

A BALLSY ADVENTURE
STARRING
BALLS!
(Flip from the back)
chik chook chook chik!
tweet! tweet!

From: PendletonWard
Yeah!
Peoo!
Peeoo!
Peeoo!
To: Jeffrey Brown
P.O. Box 120
Deerfield IL
60015-0120
FIRST CLASS
UNITED STATES POSTAL SERVICE
60015
Document Mailer

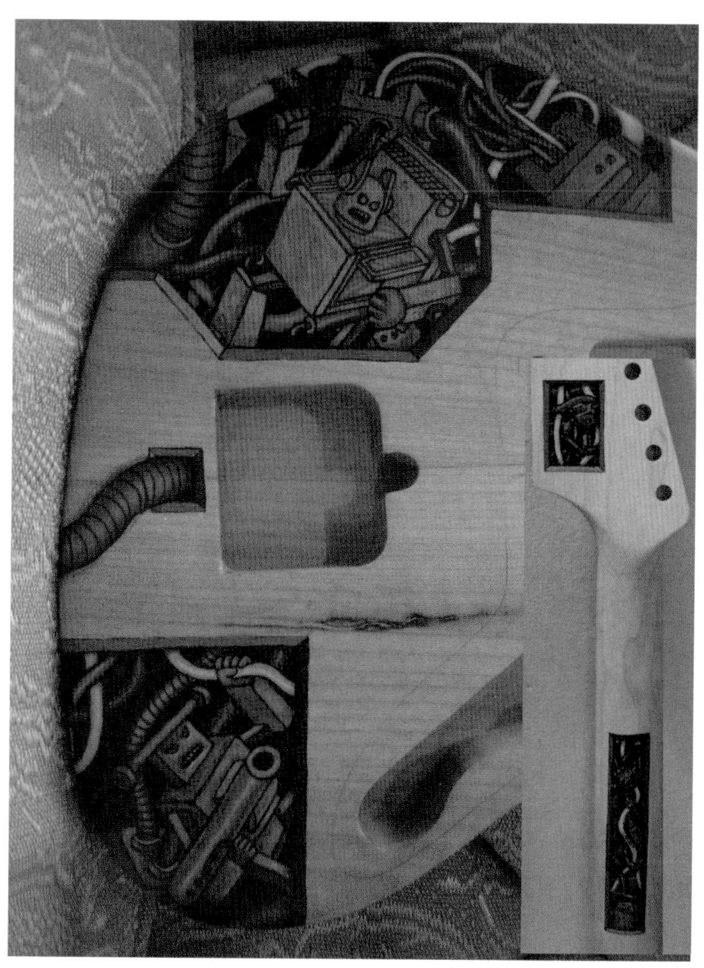

INCREDIBLE CHANGE-BOTS TWO
THU. MAY 12 7-9 PM
DESERT ISLAND
540 METROPOLITAN AVE
BROOKLYN NY 11211
(718) 388-5087
WWW.DESERTISLANDBROOKLYN.COM
READING & SIGNING
NEW YORK BOOK RELEASE CELEBRATION WITH CARTOONIST
JEFFREY BROWN
CHEE CHO CHEE CHOO CHOOK
BEW! BEW!
BDEW!
BEW!
BEW! BEW!
BEW!
CHEE CHOO
FRI. MAY 13 6-9 PM
SCOTT EDER GALLERY
18 BRIDGE ST #2-i
BROOKLYN NY 11201
(718) 797-1100
WWW.SCOTTEDERGALLERY.COM
CHANGE-BOTS
ART SHOW
OPENING RECEPTION
POSSIBLY THE MOST AWKWARD SHAPE-CHANGING ALIEN ROBOTS EVER RETURN TO EARTH IN AN ALL NEW COMIC ADVENTURE
CHEE CHOO CHEE CHOOK
MORE CHANGE-BOTS AT:
WWW.TOPSHELFCOMIX.COM
MORE JEFFREY BROWN AT:
WWW.JEFFREYBROWNCOMICS.COM

INCREDIBLE CHANGE-BOTS ~~JEFFREY BROWN~~ RETURNS TO ~~COMIX REVOLUTION~~ EARTH

JEFFREY BROWN, WHO IS NOT A ROBOT, IS THE BESTSELLING AUTHOR OF DARTHVADER AND SON AND JEDI ACADEMY, AS WELL AS NUMEROUS AUTOBIOGRAPHICAL COMICS (CLUMSY, A MATTER OF LIFE). HE LIVES IN CHICAGO WITH HIS WIFE AND TWO SONS.

JEFFREYBROWNRQ@HOTMAIL.COM

A SPECIAL THANKS TO ALL THE MEMBERS OF THE OFFICIAL INCREDIBLE CHANGE-BOTS FAN CLUB!

ORIGINAL CHANGE-BOTS ARTWORK AVAILABLE FROM SCOTT EDER GALLERY

WWW.SCOTTEDERGALLERY.COM